BROKEN AND SCREWED

TIJAN

Edited: AW Editing

Proofread: Kara Hildebrand

Cover designer: Hart & Bailey Design Co

1

When I got to the bonfire, the smell of fire and booze filled the air. Underneath was the smell of sweat. My nose wrinkled, and I grimaced but headed toward it. The guys had been partying all day since it was the last day of school. I was glad I didn't smell anything worse.

People swarmed in the woods as I continued toward wherever the fire would be. That was where my friends would be. Angie and Marissa liked to be the center of attention. Angie was the willowy blonde with a model's look. Her blue eyes seemed to launch out of her body. They were intense, smoky, and had ensnared most of the male population in our school. And Marissa rivaled her in the looks department. She was petite, with jet-black hair, dark almond eyes, and a personality that dubbed her Sullivan High School's man-eater. Even though we had finished our junior year and had three months of summer before we started our reign as seniors, I knew they wanted to start early. Those two were ready for the senior girls to leave so they could take the crown as the queens of our school.

"Alex!"

I couldn't stop a chuckle as Angie leaned over her boyfriend's shoulder and waved at me. She was so eager that she tipped forward and fell down his body and to the floor. She'd been standing on a truck and her movement sent a jerking movement underneath the rest of the girls who danced there. They screamed, grabbing on to anything to steady them. A group of guys stood around the truck. Some of the guys were ogling the girls, but some of them were chatting with their friends. More than a few jumped forward and couldn't hide their smirks when the girls grabbed them for balance.

Justin looked down at Angie on the ground, sighed, and continued talking with his friend.

"Alex!" Her shout turned into a whine, and I took her hand so I could haul her back to her feet. "I'm so embarrassed."

"You shouldn't be," I said. She'd done it enough times over the past year since she had started drinking. Then I glanced around. "Where's Marissa?"

"Where else?" Her tone turned snippy. "Trying to hit on your man. I don't know why she even tries. He doesn't want a girlfriend since he broke up with Sarah. Everyone can see that Jesse Hunt is the hit 'em and quit 'em guy this year. Seriously. He's hooked up with someone at every single party." She threw her arm around in a circle, and her voice rose a notch. "And everyone also knows that if he's going to date someone, it's going to be you."

The slight enjoyment I had when I first got to the party died. "Stop, Angie. Jesse and I aren't even friends. We're nothing."

She snorted.

"And if he were going to date someone, it would be Sarah. It wouldn't be me. He was with her for three years, remember? Those type of feelings don't vanish."

She snorted again, and then her chest heaved a few times before she crossed her arms. "I'm going to get more beer. You want any?"

I shook my head.

She left even before she saw my response, but she knew I didn't drink. The only two times I ever had any alcohol were the two times I got wasted. Both nights intermingled with harsh memories, memories I didn't even want to think about ever again.

"Alex!"

This time it was Marissa. She had a bright smile on her face as she hurried around a group. She held a cup of beer in one hand and was wiping her face with the other as she stopped next to me. She panted for a second but then flipped her black locks over her shoulder. Her hand went to her hip and, just like that, her pose could've been in a magazine.

"Hey." I was half warm, half cautious. Was she going to talk about Jesse? He'd been her obsession for the last month. I knew she didn't want to really date him, but she did want to sleep with him. Marissa had harbored feelings for him most of our lives. She never uttered a word to me until the last two months when she realized that Jesse and I were more strangers than what we had been.

She latched on to my arm. I fought from cringing from her beer breath as she fanned herself. "Okay, first: Jesse is an ass."

I relaxed. Finally.

"But, holy cow, that makes him so super hot. Am I weird? I must be wired backward. I don't know, but I want him even more. I swear. Can you talk to him? Tell him I'm good in bed. No, wait. He has to know I am. I mean, hello." She frowned, and her eyes crinkled together. "Wait. What was I talking about?"

"Marissa."

"What?" She perked up. Her nails dug into my arm.

"Let go of my arm."

"Oh!" Her eyes went wide again. "Oh my gosh! I am so sorry, Alex. Did I hurt you? Please tell me I didn't. I'm such an idiot. What was I talking about before?"

I peered closer. She didn't look that drunk.

"Oh, that's right!" Her whole body jerked up in an excited spasm. She clapped her hand to her cheek. "Please talk to Jesse. I know you say you don't want to. I know you say you're not friends with him, but I know you are. I know you both are still close, so do you think you could put in a good word for me?"

"I . . ." I had no words. This was more forward than she'd ever been before. She had to have been drunk because the alternate option was that my best friend was incredibly insensitive to me. Had she forgotten about the last year? Or why Jesse and I weren't close anymore?

And then someone threw their beer on her. She was soaked in an instant. Her mouth fell open. Anger filled her face, along with shock, but her eyes were wide as she turned. Angie stood there with a smug smile and an empty cup. She waved it at Marissa before her hand fell to her hip. Both of them faced off against each other. Angie stepped close. She was taller and looked down her nose at Marissa.

"Are you kidding me? You did not just ask Alex to put in a good word with Jesse for you? Are you serious? Seriously?"

"You bitch!" Marissa screeched. She flung her hands in the air, as if she weren't sure what to do with them.

"Guys." I started to step between them.

I was hauled back by Justin, who bypassed me to grab Angie's shoulders. He turned her away, but sent a scathing look at Marissa as he did.

"What?" Angie snapped at him.

His eyes flickered once. A dark look was in them and her hands fell back down. She took a breath, looked at me, and took another breath.

I looked away. I didn't know what I was supposed to do. Comfort her? She was wrong. It'd been too much for her to ask, but she had a beer thrown on her because of her question, which seemed like enough punishment.

"I'm sorry, Alex. I wasn't thinking about you." Marissa's voice was small but loud enough for me to hear.

I took a deep breath. My stomach settled again, and I shrugged. "It's okay."

"It's not. I was a being a selfish bitch. I forgot . . ."

My heart pounded. What was she going to say?

"Never mind. Do you want something to drink?"

I let out a deep breath of relief. She hadn't said it. And, like Angie, she left before I could reply. They both knew me so well.

Justin took Angie back to his truck, and they climbed inside. Her arms flew around. Her face kept switching from outrage to fury, and Justin kept patting her back. I stood there. I still had no idea what to do.

Angie and Justin would get heated, both of them were so honest and open that fights were inevitable. They always made up in the morning. When I saw Marissa with some of her cheer-leading friends, I knew it would be sooner than that. She was biting her lip as she cast concerned looks toward Angie. She sent a few toward me, but her eyes fluttered and she looked away.

I made the decision to leave. This party wasn't for me, not that night, not with him there.

A few girls called out good-byes when they saw that I was leaving, but no one stopped me. No one dared, because the truth was that I wasn't close to any of them anymore. I had been. A year ago, I was one of the popular girls. It was why I had become friends with Angie and Marissa. No one could rival us when we were together.

My phone buzzed as I neared my car. I pulled my phone out and saw the text from Marissa.

Marissa: I'm sorry. I really am. Please don't be mad at me. I'm really, really, really sorry if I hurt you. I'm so stupid some-times. Ok. All the time. This time. I was stupid this time. I'll make it r8t with Angie too. Promise. Breakfast in the am? Barnies?

Me: Sounds good. Call when u wake up.

Marissa: R U mad? R U hurt?

I heaved another breath. Was I mad? No. That was Marissa, she didn't think sometimes. Was I hurt? On this night, I couldn't breathe without hurting. I should've replied, told a lie to my friend, but I didn't. I pocketed my phone and kept my head down as I got to the car.

Everything slowed to a halt after that.

Nothing happened. No one made a sound. No one moved. There were no animals in the background, no smell that warned me, but tingles raced down my spine and I knew.

I looked up, swallowing over a knot.

There he was, Jesse Hunt.

His dark eyes penetrated me from across the ten yards that separated us. His black hair had been buzzed since that afternoon. His lips were curved in a sneer, and he was sitting on my car's trunk. His knees were pulled up and his feet rested on the bumper. He had on a sleeveless black shirt that was ripped at the ends. The tattoos on his arms seemed even darker from the moonlight. They were highlighted against his skin, which was a golden tan.

"What are you doing here?" I sounded hoarse.

My heart was pounding. I couldn't get enough air.

His top lip curved upward in a smile, but he still kept the sneer on his face. I never knew how he could do that, but he had perfected it by the time we hit junior high. "What? You got those virginal panties on now?" His eyes flashed a warning to me. "What do you think I'm doing here?"

I swung away. Why could he affect me so much?

"Hey!" He raised his voice a notch. "It's the big night for us, Alex. Come on. Who else would I be with tonight? Only you and me. We're the only ones."

I lowered my head. He was right. My heart slowed a bit. No

one else could understand. No one else had loved Ethan like we had.

But that didn't mean I wanted to think about my big brother at that moment. So, I swung back and rushed out, "I saw Sarah at the bonfire. She looks pretty." I wet my lips. When had they gone so dry? "Do you think you'll ever get back together with her? I think she still loves you."

He stared at me for a moment and then snorted. When he raised his hand, I saw the flask for the first time. He was drunk. Of course, he was drunk. I blinked back rapid tears. He only talked to me when he was drunk. Though, there were tons of times when he ignored my calls, my looks, or my pleas for any comfort he could've provided when he was drunk, too.

"Are you serious?" He rolled his eyes, and for some reason, it seemed savage when it came from him. He fixed me with another penetrating stare. "Come on, Alex. What are we doing here?"

"You're on *my* car."

He snorted again and raised the flask once more. "It's Ethan's car."

"He gave it to me."

I tensed, ready for a sharp rebuke, but it never came. Silence. My eyes snapped to his, and I was surprised to see that he wasn't looking at me. He had turned away. I could see his Adam's apple bobbing up and down. The image of it took my breath away. He was beautiful in that moment. The moon was behind him, casting its light over him. When he looked back, he draped both his arms on his knees. His head hung down.

His shoulders drooped as he took a breath. Hearing the shuddering inhale from him, I clasped my eyes closed.

I heard the pain in him. My own matched his, and I wanted to go to him. But that was how it happened the last time. Nothing good came out of that except more suffering.

I felt my wall crumble and whispered, "I'm tired of hurting, Jesse."

He looked back up. The cockiness was gone. The anger still burned in his eyes, but he had stuffed it down. I knew it was there, though. But it didn't keep me away. His torment was on the surface, and he let me see that.

Tears burst from my dam. I couldn't stop them.

"It's the exact time that it happened, you know. Right now. It's 11:05. June second."

The pain suffocated me, but I couldn't turn away. I nodded with my throat full. "I know."

Jesse sighed again and stretched his legs down. He slid off the trunk and leaned against it. The moonlight flashed over his flask as he raised it again. As I heard it empty, he tossed it aside and crossed his arms over his chest. Even though Jesse was lean, his biceps bulged from the movement. He had always worked out, but since Ethan died, he had doubled his time there.

"My God. I fucking loved that guy."

A hand reached inside me and squeezed my heart. More tears streamed from my eyes. I was helpless to stop them, but I choked out, "I know."

"Drive me home?"

My eyes closed again, and I wrapped my arms around myself. There it was. That was the request I knew was coming. My heart thundered while I tried to think clearly. And then I said, "Yes."

The corners of his lips curved up, just slightly.

We didn't speak after that. We didn't need to. I went to the driver's side. He went to the passenger's side. We didn't speak as I drove past his black Ferrari or when we pulled up to the mansion his father had built when Jesse's mother had been dying. As we walked through the hallways, up the stairs, and to his back bedroom, my heart was calm. I was calm, and that made me not calm.

I shouldn't have been calm.

Jesse went to his bar and poured vodka into a glass. He slid it across the counter to me. I picked it up and waited until he poured one for himself.

It was the third time we'd done this. Ethan's funeral. Ethan's birthday, and tonight, which was the anniversary of the day Ethan's first car wrapped itself around a tree. He had died a year ago and nothing was the same.

2

W hen I woke, I rolled over and wasn't surprised to see Jesse beside me. Images of the night flashed in my head as I relived the erotic moments. There was a bittersweet taste in my mouth. I couldn't stop myself from looking at his back. He was turned away from me with his arms bunched around the pillow under his head. He was on his stomach and I could see the sculpture he had created over the last year. He'd been ripped before, but he was defined, molded, and a piece of art now.

I sighed and wet my lips. The night had been one big blur of blind primal need. A carnal lust took over when I was near him, and that was the problem. Jesse hated me. He needed me on the nights when neither of us could escape Ethan's ghost, but the next morning would be another story.

As he stirred, I hurried out of the bed and dressed. When I couldn't find my shirt, I spied a sweatshirt on the chair and grabbed it.

"What the fuck are you doing?"

The savagery in his voice stilled my hand for just a second. Then I turned around as I pulled the sweatshirt over my head and gulped. He sat on the edge of the bed with clear hate in his eyes. "What?"

The small hope I'd had for morning pleasantries, maybe more, died inside. I looked away as I felt tears coming. I shoved them down, deep down, and hardened inside as I looked back.

He still glared at me, but the loathing had been blanketed. Slightly. He gestured to the sweatshirt. "That's mine. You can't have it."

"Are you serious? I don't know where my shirt is. I need a shirt."

He rolled his eyes and stood. His stomach muscles contracted from the movement, and his arms bulged for a moment before then went back to his lean build. Then he disappeared into his closet. He came out a second later with a different sweatshirt in hand and threw it at me. "You can keep this one."

It was white with a green four-leaf clover on the front. "How generous."

He flashed a smirk and rolled his shoulders back. "Whatever. Go in your bra for all I care." He stuffed the other sweatshirt in a ball and tossed it across the room. When it landed on the bed, I gasped as I saw the front for the first time. I launched for it.

He caught my wrists in his.

"That's my brother's! I want it."

My body was pressed against his as I strained for the shirt behind him, but he held my hands above my head and nudged me backward with his hips.

"No!"

He kept going with his head down. I tensed as I felt his lips skim my shoulder, and then I realized I was against a wall. Body aligned with mine, he leaned closer. His hips pressed against mine, his chest was against mine. Slowly, my hands separated, and he slid them down against the wall. They curved behind me with him still holding on to them.

I breathed deeply. I was trying to calm down, which was useless.

His lips softly touched my shoulder again. His hand curved over my waist, skimmed up my arm, and cupped the side of my face. He tilted my chin so I was forced to look at him and then sighed. His pain was evident. It shimmered on the surface, but he shook his head. He rasped out, "I'm keeping it."

My eyes clasped shut.

"I'm sorry. I really am."

I felt his coldness before he stepped back. He had already retreated behind a wall. I looked up but wasn't surprised when there was no emotion on his face. The moments when he allowed me in were fleeting. I wondered when he would stop altogether.

"Do you need a ride to your car?" My voice was hoarse.

"I'll call a buddy."

I jerked my head in a nod. We were done. Our needs had been scratched for the night. As I left, an empty feeling filled me once more. I knew it would stay there until Ethan's birthday, when Jesse would let me in once again.

The mansion was just as I remembered it. Dark and cold. There were paintings on the walls, all of them in dark colors. A few sculptures had been placed in corners, but none of them were happy. All of them seemed sad and depressed. It wasn't until I was almost to the front door that I realized none of the windows were open. All the curtains were pulled shut. It was as if the sunlight wasn't allowed inside.

When I left the front door and saw my car in the open garage, I suppressed a shiver. Jesse's home was big, cold, and empty. I now understood why he lived with us most of the time since seventh grade until last year. His mother had died when he was in eighth grade, but I never considered what his home had been like. The few times I heard him mention his father, he never referred to him as Dad, just 'the dick.' When I drew close to my car and opened the door, I saw the cars lined up beside it. A

Lamborghini, a Porsche, another Ferrari. Jesse only drove his black Ferrari, so those must be his father's. My dad drove a Sable. Something told me our fathers were very different.

My phone beeped, and I knew it was my alarm without having to look. I had to be at work within the hour. As I got home and rushed inside, my mom was in the kitchen. The aroma of coffee filled the air, and I heard the coffee maker still brewing. Before I slipped upstairs, I peeked around the corner. My mom still had her robe on, and she stood at the sink with a cup of coffee in her hand. I knew without seeing her face there was a blank stare in her eyes. It had been there for a year.

As I watched, her head dropped down, her shoulders sagged, and she placed the mug to the side. A disgusted sigh came from her before she reached inside a bottom cabinet and poured something in her coffee.

It wasn't creamer.

That empty feeling doubled inside me. I went to my room. My arms and legs were numb, but I tried to shower and dress in a hurry. When I went back down the stairs, my mom was still at the sink. Her mug was raised back to her lips. When I went outside and looked through the window, I knew I was right. A blank stare was on her face. I raised my hand to her, but there was no reaction. Her eyes never blinked. She never wavered in her stance.

So I left.

When I got to the food court in the mall, I slipped underneath the counter at the coffee shop. Ben pivoted at my abrupt arrival and had an eyebrow arched high before I even met his gaze. I cringed at the curiosity in them and steeled myself.

"What?"

His mouth gaped open at me for a second before he snapped it shut in a dramatic fashion. Then he pointed over my shoulder. "Your BFF is here with all his godly basketball buddies." Then he gestured toward the trendy clothes shop closest across from us.

"And I think Casey and her winos are going to move in for the kill."

I cringed again at the sarcastic pleasure he laced each of his words with. "Sometimes, Ben, you're too interested in everyone else."

He shuddered and clasped a hand to his heart. "I cannot believe you would dare say such a thing."

I rolled my eyes and filled a coffee for myself.

He groaned as I put the lid on and sipped it. "How you drink that without sugar or cream is beyond me. It's foul, Alexandra. Foul, I say!"

I was about to respond when a customer approached our Coffee Hut, and I took care of her order. A steady line formed after that. It was an hour later before I was able to drink my own coffee.

Ben reached over me for a lid as he handed the last order away, but then he checked me with his hip. "He's still there. And he keeps looking over here."

I knew who Ben was referring to. He was under the same assumption as Angie that Jesse and I were meant to be. We weren't. Obviously. Yet, I couldn't help but to look over, and when I did, I was captivated by him. His friends were laughing around him, but Jesse stared straight at me.

I sighed and looked down. I couldn't handle him, not now, not after last night and how he basically threw me out this morning.

Ben gasped and then he bent close to my ear before he hissed, "He's coming over here."

And he was. A few of his friends glanced over, but no one stopped him. They went back to their stories or lounging in a cool way, the stance that jocks perfected long ago.

His jeans rode low on his hips, but he had a simple black shirt on. It didn't matter how simple his clothes were. He always looked beautiful. My stomach crumbled and shattered into pieces as I admitted that last thought, but then he was almost at the Coffee Hut.

"Hi, Jesse!" Casey stopped in front of him. Her hands were poised on her hips, which were prominent under skin-tight white jeans and a pink top that fit like a second skin. She flipped her platinum blonde hair over one shoulder and laughed in a flirtatious manner.

Her friends gathered behind her. All of them looked just like her, and Ben had once whispered that he thought their secret mission was to copy the leader until they took her down. When I caught a few of their hungry gazes, I wondered if it were true. If they waited in line until it was their turn to be the leader. When that happened, what guy would they go after?

Ben hissed again beside me. "Succubi. They're all succubi."

I nudged him as one of the girls flashed us a dark look. "If they are, you don't want to take on a demonic beauty queen."

He shifted to the side and lowered his voice. "That's true, very true."

Jesse had moved around Casey, and she followed behind him. As he neared the Coffee Hut, she looked up. The light in her eyes dimmed and her smile slipped. "Oh. Hi, Alex."

I gave her a polite smile but gritted my teeth on the inside. "Hi, Casey."

"How are Angie and Justin doing? I heard they had a fight last night."

My eyes narrowed at her. "If they did, I'm sure they've made up by now. You know how those two are, always hot together."

She snorted and flipped her hair back again. "Whatever. They're not going to last. Justin was with me before. Everyone remembers the two of us. We were the perfect couple."

The corner of Jesse's lips twitched, and I knew what he was thinking. My eyebrow arched. "Then why'd you throw yourself at my brother?"

Casey's smirk vanished, and her eyes grew heated. "Your

brother was a good guy. And he shouldn't have been with that ditzy airhead. I was doing him a favor when I broke them up."

"And when you dropped Justin, your perfect boyfriend, at the same time?"

Her fury blasted me, and she slapped a hand down on the counter. "Hear this, Alexandra Connors. I've always liked you and I will always have a special place in my heart for Ethan, but if you piss me off, you will have me as an enemy."

I held my breath. I didn't care about anything Casey threatened, but I couldn't look away from Jesse. He had been amused at the beginning, but a wall slipped down again. The same blank mask was in place, but he reached forward and removed Casey's hand from the counter. Then he moved to stand in front of her with his back to the Coffee Hut. Her eyes snapped to his, but the slight delight that sparked drained along with the blood in her face. She grew pale and backed away.

His voice was soft. "I think you should leave."

A chill went down my spine. He was quiet, but there was a lethal undertone to his voice. Casey reacted to it.

Everyone reacted to it, even Ben, whose eyes widened as he backed against the farthest corner we had. His hands shook, but he pressed them behind him and turned away. I caught the blush on his chubby cheeks and grinned.

Then I turned and my smile left.

Jesse placed my shirt on the counter. He lifted dead eyes to me. "I found it."

"Thanks."

A few of Casey's friends arched their necks to see what he had put on the counter, so I snagged it quickly and stuffed it underneath the counter. I knew my own cheeks were red, and I looked away. "Did you want something else?"

I couldn't look. I shouldn't have been embarrassed, but I couldn't help it. He had returned my top in a public setting, at my job, at the mall. I groaned as I heard Ben's sharp intake of breath, but then I noticed the lack of response from Jesse and looked back.

He was gone.

He was already at his table with his friends.

"That. Was. Awesome!" Ben breathed out and jumped to my side.

He sounded so excited, but the embarrassment was gone for me. Oh, no. Instead, I kicked myself. I should've known he wasn't coming over to chat with me or see how I was. He found my shirt. Of course, that was the only reason he came over.

I felt the onslaught of a few tears. Hell no. I wasn't going to cry over him. He didn't deserve it, and I knew that whatever twisted tradition we had on the days that celebrated Ethan's birth and death was done.

As I watched him stand with his friends, I knew I couldn't allow it to happen again. He didn't give me a second look. He walked out as if we were strangers again, which we were. And I couldn't forget it, even though I knew I was in love with Jesse Hunt. I always had been.

3

I saw Jesse a few more times after that, but we didn't speak or even acknowledge each other. Then, in the first week in August, Angie asked me to attend one of Justin's softball games. When I realized Jesse was on his team, it had been a shock, but it shouldn't have been. He may have been was awarded a full scholarship to Grant West University for basketball, but I knew he was talented in other sports. He and Ethan would spend hours in the backyard pitching the ball to each other. Most of the time, it was a whiffle ball, but both of them played softball and baseball during the summers.

As I watched him, I swore I felt Ethan beside me. Everything was starting to tingle inside me, and I could smell his cologne. I swallowed thickly when I felt tears start to swell up. As I continued to sit through the first game, my brother's presence was so strong. I couldn't hold the tears anymore. After the last inning when Jesse scored the winning home run, I couldn't watch him run the bases for home plate, and I left the bleachers.

"Alex!" Angie called after me, but I kept going.

I brushed some of the tears away and hid in her car until the crowd started to leave. It was twenty minutes later when I saw members of their team going toward their cars. As I hunkered down and waited for Angie, I looked up and gasped. Jesse stood in front of the car, staring at me hard. Then he blinked and the small spell was broken. I held my breath and waited. A part of me knew he would leave and not look back, but the other part of me thought he'd come to the window.

He did nothing. He stood there and stared at me.

I realized he was waiting for me to decide, so I opened the door and crawled out. My legs were unsteady as I leaned back against the car and he came around to my side.

He smelled of sweat and dirt. The front of his softball uniform was covered in the field's sand from when he had slid to the bases. Beads of sweat glistened on his forehead and drenched his hair. Then he ran a hand through it and I saw it was water instead.

"What are you doing here?" he asked in a low voice. He had no emotion, as always.

I took a deep breath to calm my nerves. "Angie wanted to watch Justin. I came for support."

His jaw clenched, and he rubbed a hand over his chin.

Everything in me was chaos, but I rasped out, "I didn't know you were on the team."

"Why would that matter?"

My eyes jerked to his. The question was real . . . genuine. I couldn't stop a snort in disbelief. "Are you kidding? You hate me."

"Oh." Then he looked away.

My nerves were stretched to the max as I waited for him to talk. I needed something, anything. I wanted to hear that he didn't hate me, but after another minute of silence, I knew it wasn't coming. My gut had been right.

When he turned back, his eyes were piercing. A dark emotion was there, but he held it back. "Come over tonight."

"What?"

"Come over tonight."

"Why? It's not Ethan's—"

But I was stopped as he stepped close. His body heat radiated off him in waves, and I held my breath. His fingers touched the side of my hip, and he lowered his lips so they were an inch from mine. He said again, "Come over tonight."

I did the only thing I was capable of doing.

I nodded.

His lips touched my forehead in a soft kiss and then he ran his thumb over my cheek before he left.

"See ya, Hunt!" Justin hollered, and I was jerked back to reality.

I knew my entire face was red, but I couldn't ignore Angie's silence. I knew she had witnessed that and I knew she was biding her time until we were alone. And because I didn't want to undergo an interrogation, I did something I hadn't done in a year and a half.

I twisted around and shouted, "Jesse!"

He stopped and looked back, waiting.

"Alex?" Angie asked in a soft voice.

My heart was racing, but I took a deep breath. "Can I get a ride with you?"

He had pulled his black shades back on so his eyes were blocked, but he didn't respond for a moment. Then his shoulder jerked up in a shrug and relief exploded inside me. I trembled from the onslaught of it but grabbed my purse and bolted around the car.

"Wha—huh?" Justin glanced at his girlfriend. "Ang?"

Her mouth snapped shut and she folded her arms.

I ignored it all and picked up my pace to catch up to Jesse, who had already started walking to his car. He didn't wait for me until he got into the Ferrari. My fingers fumbled for the door handle. I cursed after the sixth try. It still wouldn't open. He leaned across and opened it from the inside for me. When I climbed in, the air conditioner was already working and blasted me with cool air, but I glanced at him. I expected some scathing joke at my clumsiness, but there was nothing. His shades were in place and his lips were flat as he gunned the engine and we soared out of the parking lot.

When he went past my street, I looked over in surprise. "Where are we going?"

He didn't answer. He kept driving.

Then we went past his street. I sat forward. "Seriously, Jesse. Where are we going?"

The corner of his lip twitched, but he asked in a low voice, "How are your folks?"

"What?"

"Don and Shelby. Your mom and dad. How are they?"

He hadn't asked about my parents since . . . I blinked. It'd been before Ethan's death. A different tension filled my body and I was rigid from my eyeballs to my toenails. "Why are you asking?" I couldn't keep out the anger and I grimaced against it. I hadn't wanted him to hear that.

He looked over this time, but didn't say anything for a second. When he returned to the street, I caught the slight frown on his face. "Is something wrong at home?"

That got a laugh out of me. "Are you kidding?"

The frown vanished. There was nothing again.

I couldn't stop another laugh and the sound was ugly to my own ears. "No, Jesse. My family's great. Don and Shelby have mourned the loss of their son in their own way, and me, I'll be just fine. I'm just screwing his best friend at times."

And then I stopped. I had so much more to say, but I held it back. What good would it do? It'd only scare him away. At that confession, my heart shifted a bit. I felt it shrink or move or slip further away. I was with Jesse with the hopes that he'd give me anything, even a crumb of his touch. I was that girl. I sat back and stared straight ahead. I was that girl, just hoping for anything.

Shame filled me.

Jesse didn't say anything more until the car started to slow down. I saw that we were at the ocean. When we got out, the salt in the air stung my eyes. That was why I was crying again. It had to be the reason. But I didn't have time to continue my own lie as Jesse was already down a hill. I followed behind on the path and slowed as I watched where he was leading us. When he sat on the sand where there was no one around, I stopped in my tracks.

Why there? Why then? What was he doing?

"Would you stop thinking and sit beside me?" Jesse patted the spot beside him and I obliged. Of course I would oblige. Where else was I going to go?

We sat in silence for a while, longer than I could handle. My heart kept pounding. It got louder the longer we sat until I thought I was going to burst.

Then he sighed. He had his arms draped over his knees as he stared out at the ocean. "Your brother and I were supposed to go surfing here last year after graduation. We made the plans that day. It was our stupid way of celebrating together, even though Sarah wanted me to have that damn dinner with her parents. I didn't go to the party that night."

I looked down. I'd forgotten that fact.

He took a deep breath and shook his head. "I'm going to Grant West, you know."

"I know."

"I won't be here anymore."

Tears filled my eyes. He hadn't been here for a long time, but I bit my tongue.

He sounded apologetic. "I don't want to talk about you and me, about—whatever. It's done. It's fine. We'll deal with it, but you've got some good friends. Angie's a good friend to you, so is Marissa. They both care about you, in their ways. So you should be okay, right?"

"Uh, what?"

He looked at me this time, but he never took the sunglasses

off. The wall was so pretty and perfect. "You have friends that'll look out for you next year. I won't be here and your folks . . . they're good parents. Hell, they raised me most of the time."

But that was when he had lost his mother and when his father became an absent one. And that was when Ethan was alive, when my parents could function as normal parents and when they still cared about the little things in life like their other child. That wasn't now and that hadn't been for a long time.

I said none of that. Instead, I gave him a small smile. "You're right. I'll be just fine."

"Your brother would want that."

Ethan would want a lot more, but I didn't say that either. I sighed. "What are you doing, Jesse?"

The wind shifted and he went with it. The cold Jesse was back in place. I was startled to realize that he had opened up to me, just a bit, but it was gone. I couldn't see through his sunglasses, but I knew his eyes were dead again. "We should go back."

And just like that, the rare moment was gone. It had slipped through my fingers and I hadn't even realized I had the chance to grasp something. When he dropped me off at home, I hesitated to ask if he still wanted me to come over that night. I didn't think I could take more of his rejection, so I waited the rest of the day at home, ignored Angie and Marissa's text messages, and dressed in something sexy.

I shouldn't have. I knew that, but as my heart pounded, I knew I couldn't stay away. He had asked. It was enough for me, so I wore a slinky black dress. It was simple, something that I could've worn to a party or to a girl's night out. I drove to his house.

My heart wouldn't stop pounding. That was my normal heart rate now. My palms were sweaty and as I knocked on his door, I didn't know what I was going to face.

When it opened, I held my breath. Mary, his housekeeper, answered. Before I could open my mouth, she held an arm out and pointed inside. When she turned and waddled away, I heard her mumble under her breath, "Always Alex, he says. Always Alex, he says."

As I walked through the mansion, the same cold feeling came to me. Goose bumps ran up and down my arms as I turned down the last hallway. His room was the last door, but when I opened it, I knew he wasn't there.

I took a shuddering breath. It rattled in my lungs and I didn't know what else to do.

Leave?

But then I couldn't look away from his bed. It was a king size. The sheets were rumpled from when he had gotten up that morning. I knew how they felt. I shivered from the need I had to curl up among them. The nights I had spent in there had been the best sleep I'd gotten. Before I had fully made my decision, I slipped off my sandals and crawled underneath his sheets. They were so soft to the touch. I nestled under them.

My body started to relax and the fatigue started to slip in. My eyelids grew heavy, but before I drifted off to sleep, I thought I saw a black shape in the doorway. But then it didn't matter and I was asleep.

"What? What is *she* doing here?!"

A shrill voice snapped me out of my sleep and I jerked upright.

"Shut up." It was a low command.

"I won't shut up! Look at her! What's she doing there, Jesse? I thought you wanted me tonight and we find *her* in your bed!"

I rubbed my eyes and tried to make sense of what woke me up.

Then I heard a curse and he snapped, "Fucking leave then."

"What?" The girl calmed down and whimpered. "But I thought—"

"I don't give a shit. Go."

And then the door shut behind them and I lay back down,

exhausted once again. It wasn't long before it opened again and I sat back up. As I yawned, Jesse stood inside the door, frowning at me.

I continued my yawn. "You told me to come over tonight."

Then he yawned and rubbed a hand over his face. There were lines of exhaustion around his eyes and for a moment, they were sad. My heart skipped a beat. I resisted the urge to pull him into my arms. But then the look vanished, and he grimaced at me. "I didn't think you'd still come."

I looked away, gathering the bedcovers around me. "You hoped I wouldn't still come."

Then he sighed. The bed sank underneath his weight as he sat against the headboard beside me. "Do you blame me?"

I swung around and really looked at him. The fatigue was back on his face, but the wall had fallen. Hope sparked inside me. It leapt like a flame in a fire that'd been smoldering. It was hungry and wanted more, but I contained it. I kept my voice under control as I asked, "Why didn't you want me to come?"

"Because I goddamn feel everything." His voice was gruff. "I'm sick of feeling, Alex. Only you. No other girl makes me feel this shit I don't want to."

And without thinking, I reached out and took his hand in mine. Our fingers slid against each other and then I nestled back underneath the covers. It wasn't long before he sighed again and scooted behind me. His arm came over my waist and one of his legs slipped between mine. When his chest started to rise and fall in a deep slumber, I allowed a small smile.

I didn't know what was in store for the future, but I didn't want to be anywhere else except in his arms. But then my gut kicked and I knew this temporary shelter would be ripped away once more.

Jesse was always ripped away from me.

4

I woke up when Jesse nudged me onto my back and then moved above me. When my eyes opened, I knew what was happening, and I wanted it. As his lips touched my neck, I wound my legs around his. Soon we were both groaning.

An hour later, after we were both spent, Jesse groaned and got up. He padded barefoot into his bathroom. His shower turned on, and I took that as my cue. Instead of my dress, I nabbed one of his larger shirts and a pair of his shorts. I knew they weren't Ethan's, so I knew Jesse wouldn't care. As soon as I was dressed, I hurried out of there.

When I got home, the place was empty as I rushed upstairs, but I was used to it. It seemed that my dad lived at his office and my mother was usually in bed at all hours of the day. I dressed for work and left, making sure I locked the door behind me.

It wasn't until I pulled into the mall's parking lot that I realized I hadn't heard the television in my parents' bedroom. Mom always fell asleep to the news. For some reason, the hairs on the back of my neck stood, but I tried to shake the uneasy feeling. I'm sure my mother was okay. She was always okay, distant but okay.

Ben arrived at the Coffee Hut at the same time as I did. It

didn't take long for the other two girls to leave and we got comfortable. It was a weekend night, so we both expected it to be slow, which it was. After an hour of not having a single customer, the sight of Angie and Marissa made me feel giddy. Ben stopped in the middle of his story, but I was okay with that. I couldn't hear much more about his dog, Mickey, who liked to hump other dogs and was the happiest English Cocker Spaniel there was in the world.

"Hey, guys!"

Both shared a look at my bright smile.

"What?" I rolled my eyes. "You guys want coffee?"

"No." Angie snorted. "We're just at the Coffee Hut to smell the merchandise, not actually to buy it."

Marissa grinned and tightened her hold on the bags in her hands.

"Where'd you guys go?" I tried to count the bags, but there were too many. I wasn't surprised. Marissa was the shopper in the group.

She shrugged and flipped her black hair over her shoulder. "Just some stores. I got a sexy outfit for school. You need to go with me next week. I've seen your wardrobe. You need something sexy for the first day."

Angie narrowed her eyes. "Where were you last night? Justin had people over, but neither of us could get a hold of you all night."

Ben sucked in his breath beside me. He started to hum from his excitement.

I shrugged. "I stayed home. I didn't feel like going out."

"But you couldn't tell me that? I texted you a million times."

Marissa arched her eyebrows and looked at Angie in surprise. She bit her lip as a frown formed.

"I know. I'm sorry. I've been out of sorts."

"You've been out of sorts for a long time," Angie snapped and crossed her arms. "What's going on with you?"

"Hey—" Marissa opened her mouth.

"I don't need a friend intervention. I'm *fine*. I've just been sad lately. Get off my back," I snapped.

"You took off with Jesse yesterday." I glared at Angie at the same moment Ben turned his eyes to me.

"You did?" his breathing picked up. He whispered underneath his breath, "That is awesome."

"You did?" Marissa's tone chilled, and she moved back a step. Her arms folded over her chest as she mirrored Angie's pose. "I thought the two of you were nothing to each other. When did this change?"

I felt caught in their sights. And something told me they both knew more than they were sharing. So, I sighed in surrender and asked, "What have you heard?"

Both girls frowned and glared at me, but Marissa was the one to answer. "Just that Casey Wright said you were in Jesse's bed last night. She left the party with him but came back an hour later majorly pissed off. And the things she was saying about you . . . if I weren't so pissed that you ditched us for him, I would've taken her out."

I froze as I heard her words.

They both knew I lied.

This was not good.

Then I looked at Angie. Her eyes had softened, but I saw the hurt in them. "I'm sorry for not telling you."

She softened even more. Her arms fell back down to her side. "It's whatever. I guess. So what's going on with you two?"

Marissa looked away.

I may have softened Angie but Marissa wasn't going to budge. I only hoped that I wouldn't lose her friendship because of it. "I thought you supported the idea of Jesse and me."

"I did, but you'd been distant and even quieter since his graduation two months ago." Her hands lifted in the air. "What do you want from me? You've been off since Ethan died, and you were

finally becoming a little more normal until that night. Since you
left with Jesse—"

"Wait. How do you know that?"

"I saw you, and then you never responded to my text. When I
came out to make sure you were okay. I saw the two of you and he
got in your car. It doesn't take a genius, Alex. I knew what you did.
And you never came to Barnies the next day for breakfast."

"And you've been so distant from us since then. We can't even
depend on you to hang out with us. I mean, Justin had a party last
night and you wouldn't respond to our text messages."

Ben harrumphed beside me. "She doesn't text me back,
either."

I swung around. "You texted me last night?"

He shrugged and edged to the side. "I would've. I thought
about it."

I continued to stare at him.

He looked away and busied himself with a customer that had
approached on the side. "Hi! How can I help you?"

I turned back to my friends. "I'm sorry. I am. I just . . . I don't
know what to say."

"So are you guys together or what? Casey said she got booted
out by him. He took one look at you and practically threw her out
of his home. Granted, I loved hearing that she got booted on her
ass, but . . ." Marissa trailed off and shared another dark look with
Angie. She took a breath, as if to ready herself. "But what's going
on? Are you guys dating?"

I looked away. What could I say? No, we weren't. My friends
would lecture me on how I needed to be a strong woman. I
couldn't give up the jewels for nothing, but they didn't know what
it was like. I could escape with him, only him. It wouldn't be the
same with anyone else. I would feel empty. I did feel empty with
everyone else, even spending time with people.

Jesse understood.

Then I lifted my shoulders in a helpless shrug. "No, we aren't together. I don't know what else to say other than that Jesse loved him, too."

"Oh!" Angie's eyes went wide.

Marissa looked horrified.

"Oh my gawd. I didn't even think about that." Angie surged forward. Her hand clamped down on mine where it was on the counter. She squeezed it. "I am so sorry, Alex. We—we didn't even think about that." Her shoulders sagged. "I'm a horrible friend. I should've thought about that."

"Yeah, well, don't worry about it." My tone was casual, but I couldn't ignore the guilt in my stomach. It spread throughout me. I looked anywhere but at my friends. I shouldn't have pulled away and I knew I had. Angie was right. Since that graduation night, I had steadily stopped responding to them and hanging out with them.

"Okay, um . . ." Marissa still bit her lip, but she forced a cheery voice out. "There's a thing at the baseball fields tonight. It's like a midnight tournament. Do you want to go?"

I held my breath. Did I?

"Jesse will be there." Marissa added. "The whole thing's like a good-bye to him tonight."

And that was my reminder that he had become the school's star over the last year. He went from an above average athlete to excelling where no one could touch his records. I forgot how much Jesse had achieved over the last year, but in a sense I understood. He pursued anything that would keep his mind from Ethan. I did the same, but that meant I pulled away from everyone else.

Ben gushed out, "Can I come, too?"

Both Angie and Marissa cracked a smile.

Then Angie questioned, "Alex?"

I already knew I was going. Who was I kidding? I was glutton for punishment, and seeing Jesse in his element was definitely going to be a punishment for me.

I nodded my agreement.

Ben clapped his hands together. "Oh, goody! I can't wait. I have the perfect shirt in mind."

When I got to the baseball fields that night, it was after ten. We couldn't leave until the mall closed, and Ben insisted that I drive him to his house first. He needed a ride and wanted my opinion on the jeans he had chosen to go with his perfect shirt. I didn't care. After seeing ten different jeans that had jewels on the back pockets, I finally lied and picked one. In truth, as we got out of my car and headed toward the fields, Ben didn't look half bad.

He seemed happy as I pulled into the almost full parking lot, though he wasn't really trying to hide his excitement or the huge smile on his face. He confessed that he had always wanted to attend an event with my girlfriends and me. Apparently we were the "it" girls for the next year.

I had no idea what he meant, but I nodded.

As we approached the fields, they were lit and all five of them were filled with teams. The steel bleachers in between were also filled to the maximum. The fences that separated the fields from the crowd had lounge chairs lined up two deep from the bleachers to the end of the field.

When we stepped around the concessions, I heard my name shouted and looked around.

Eric Nathan grinned at me as he gestured from inside the concessions stand.

Ben leaned close and whispered, "I knew it was true. I heard a rumor that he wanted to ask you out since his girlfriend broke up with him. He's making his move!"

I nudged him back and moved forward. "Hey, Eric."

"Hi!" He had a friendly smile on his face. As he skimmed over my shoulder and saw Ben behind me, it slipped a bit. Then he ran a hand through his sandy-blond hair. His blue eyes seemed to sparkle even more as his perfect teeth flashed me a smile. "I'm glad to see you here. I didn't know if you'd come."

"Right." I frowned at him.

"Because, you know, because Hunt is the reason for tonight, but . . ." He frowned and heaved a deep sigh. "I'm sorry. Maybe I shouldn't say anything. I don't really know what I'm talking about."

Ben hummed behind me again. His whole body vibrated and I knew he was excited as he whispered in my ear, "He's so cute. He likes you."

I shoved him backward.

"Shut up."

I glared at him and turned back to Eric, whose frown deepened, but then he shook it off and gave me another grin. "You want a soda?"

"I would love one."

I stayed there for a while. Eric was nice. He was a jock from my grade with a lot of friends. Angie and Marissa would have given him the green light. To be honest, in another time and place I might have, too. Then, I looked up and saw Jesse on the field. He had hit another home run. The crowd cheered as he rounded the bases. My heart faltered for a second.

There was no emotion on his face. His mouth was flat. His eyes were focused in front of him as he rounded each base. When he soared over home plate, his teammates met him and took their turn clapping him on the back. He had a smile on his face. There was no doubt about that, but it never reached his eyes. And no one else besides me would've known that he didn't care if he hit zero home runs or twenty.

Then his eyes met mine, and I jerked awake.

"Something wrong?" Eric asked, but his voice was at a distance.

Thirty people separated us, but it didn't matter. Jesse stared at me, and I stared back. I needed him. I hungered for him and when his eyes darkened, I knew he felt the same. Then I turned and bid my farewell to Eric. It didn't matter how nice he was. I knew where I'd be that night. A shiver of anticipation went through me. It sizzled my skin, and I felt exhilarated as I found Angie and Marissa in a group behind the players' seats.

Angie was on her feet, clapping loudly. "Come on, Justin! Come on. One more! One more, baby!"

Marissa smirked at me. "You'd think he was in the pros."

Angie flashed us a glare. "Shut up. That's my man, and I'm supporting him. You all should take lessons. This is what you do when you love someone unconditionally. You clap and cheer like a mad woman, and you don't complain one bit. That's what it's like."

"You look crazy?" I grinned at her.

Angie sobered but then rolled her eyes. "Yes, or at least that's what Justin wants. So I'm here cheering like a crazy woman. Whatever. I love that man. I'll cheer until I get arrested if that's what he wants."

I took the lawn chair beside Marissa, and we watched Angie more than the game. She whooped, booed, and yelled with the best of them. I thought she was going to break out in her own cheer at one point, but when she collapsed in her lawn chair, I sighed in relief. I didn't know if I would've cheered with her or hid from embarrassment.

Ben had gone to see some of his friends, but he returned for the last few innings and took the seat beside Marissa. When Justin's team won seventeen to five, no one was surprised. Jesse had been on the team. We picked up our lawn chairs and waited to find out where the next game would commence.

Close to midnight, I returned to the concessions stand. The line had tripled since we first arrived.

"Well, hello, Jesse's slut!"

I froze for a split second, but turned. Casey Wright gave me a smug smirk as she stood with her friends behind her. All of them had their hair up in braids or styled to look cute as they wore baseball caps. And, of course, they wore tee shirts tied underneath their breasts and low-riding jeans.

When I saw her shirt had Jesse's number, I took a breath. What was going to happen here?

Eric had popped his head out of the concession stand when he saw me, but now he faltered. I knew he had heard her.

"What do you want, Casey?"

She snorted in disbelief. "Are you kidding me? Leave Jesse alone."

I sighed. When would she learn? "He's going away, Casey. You have no shot."

"And you do?"

"I never said I did."

She snorted again and flipped her hair over her shoulder. Some of it trailed out from the back of her cap. Her emerald eyes were disgusted. "Are you kidding me, Alex? I told you what would happen if you got me as an enemy."

"Oh yeah? And what's that?" Angie surged forward from behind me. Her hands found her hips and her lips were in a snarl. Marissa was right next to her. Both of them looked fierce.

Casey eyed them wearily. "Really? The three of you against me?"

Marissa snorted. "Do you really think you're all that? You're second line, Casey. Get behind us."

Her eyes snapped in irritation. "I am *not* second line. How dare you say that?"

Marissa's tiny body was tense, and she looked ready to hurl herself at the girl, but she threw her chin forward. Her arms crossed over her chest and she glared. The loathing in her eyes sent me backwards a step. "Are you fucking kidding me? You're *always* second line. You got second line in cheerleading. You're in the honors class, not the highest honors. You get Bs when I get

As. I get the captains and you're lucky to get a starter. Do I need to keep going?" She threw her arms wide. "You're second best, Casey. You always will be. Just get used to it and settle back. Shut the hell up, bitch."

It was at that time that I grew tired of the conversation. Confrontations happened all the time, but it didn't matter. They had stopped mattering when I lost my brother. It might've sounded cliché, but I no longer cared. It was all stupid and senseless.

I edged toward the end of the crowd that had formed and slipped around the corner. I flattened myself against the side of the concessions building and took a few deep breaths. None of it mattered. Nothing. There was more to life. I took a few more deep breaths and tried to calm myself down, but my hands wouldn't stop shaking. Why was my breathing so labored? Maybe it did matter.

"Hey."

I calmed instantly and stopped.

Jesse was at the far end of the building. He stepped closer, but he reeked of sweat. Then he took off his cap and shook out his sweaty hair. Droplets splattered on me and he grinned. "Sorry about that."

I ducked my head to hide my grin. I shouldn't have been so happy to see him.

Then he leaned an arm beside me, giving me a cocky smirk. "You left real quick this afternoon."

I jerked a shoulder up. My cheeks were still aflame.

"A guy who was more insecure might've thought he wasn't good in bed."

I choked out a laugh but smothered it quickly before rolling my eyes at him. "Are you serious?"

"Yeah." He edged closer.

My smile wiped away. I saw he was. I stood straighter.

His mouth curved up in a grin, but it dipped down again. The smile was faulty. "Are you okay?"

"Yeah."

He nodded and let out a breath in relief. "Good. That's good."

"Are you?"

"What?" He looked back up, surprised.

"Are you okay?" My grin was precious.

Then he choked out a laugh. "Yeah, I'm okay. Why wouldn't I be?"

"Because you feel."

His hand caught my shirt, and I closed my eyes. His hand was so close to me. It curved inward so he could pull me closer. His other hand touched the base of my neck and his fingers spread upward to cup my chin and lift it so I looked in his eyes. He had moved even closer. Then he whispered as his lips brushed against mine. "I only feel with you."

"I know." My heart was racing. It pounded in every cell of my body. I was alive in his touch.

His eyes dipped to my lips.

Desire blasted within me. I grew wet between my legs.

He moved closer, pressing against me as he whispered. "Ethan wouldn't want this."

I curved a hand up and around the back of his head. This time I was the one who held him in place and I anchored him to look in my eyes. When they snapped to mine, I breathed out, "He's the reason for this."

And then his lips were on mine. I surged against him, and as I opened my mouth, I didn't want to be anywhere else. When Jesse left, a part of me would go with him, but until then, I let myself go. I succumbed to him, and it wasn't long before he swept an arm around me and held me against him. We both knew where we would end up that night.

5

That was my last night with Jesse. He left for Grant West a few weeks later, and I got ready for my senior year in high school. It wasn't the same as last year. So much time had passed. Last summer, I was still reeling from Ethan's death. I was trying to figure out how to move on, to survive, but this year was a bit different.

I existed before.

I was trying to live now.

As I walked into school on my first day as a senior, I couldn't stop the sadness inside me. Ethan had been a great senior. He had led where Jesse was supposed to take over. Then both of them were going to room together at the university. While he would never fulfill their promise to attend college together, Jesse fulfilled the plan of ruling his year being a senior. He stopped being my friend and staying at my home, he excelled in every way that he and Ethan planned. He took over in sports. He excelled in his studies and graduated as the valedictorian. And he received seven full scholarships because of his work.

He did it all by mastering the one thing I couldn't seem to get a handle on. His emotions. When I was lost in them, drowning in all sadness able to barely hold my head above water long enough to exist, he perfected the art of not feeling them at all.

He had gone from a nice guy to a badass womanizer.

Jesse had left our school with the reputation of a player, but after this past summer, I wasn't sure if he had wanted that reputation.

Though we hadn't talked much that last night, our time together hadn't been just for intercourse. We had made love. It had been slow. It had been tender. And when morning came, neither of us had wanted to see that first ray of sunlight. Even when we had, we both ignored it. I had stayed in his bed through my shift at the mall. His phone had gone off, but he ignored it as well. And then during that evening, I finally pulled myself from his bed.

I was the one that had left, but he hadn't argued with me.

We'd stared at each other as the door closed, and then it had been done.

I took a deep breath as I had gone to my car. My body had been numb that evening. The feeling hadn't left. It was still with me.

The sounds of lockers slamming penetrated it and I lifted my head.

Angie was there with Justin. They both waved, but it was perfunctory, and they went right back to their cuddling. Marissa was at the end of the hallway, dressed in her cheerleading uniform for the football game that night. Eric wasn't far away as he stood with his friends, most of whom were on the football team. He wasn't dressed in his jersey, and it took me a moment to remember that he played basketball and not football. He would've been on Jesse's team.

As I went to my locker, both of my friends separated from their groups and headed toward me. A part of me felt bad. They shouldn't have to stop their fun to make sure I was okay. That was something I felt they'd been doing for over a year now.

"Hey!" Angie gave me a bright smile. She had her books in her hand and hugged them to her chest. "What class do you have first?"

"I don't. It's my free period."

"Oh." Her smile faltered. "I have college biology. I thought you were going to take that with me?"

I shook my head. "I took it last year."

"You did?"

I nodded. "Yeah. I—uh—school was all I kind of focused on last year, you know?"

"Oh right. I forgot." She blinked a few times and then nudged Marissa.

"So, hey!" She jumped forward. Her cheerleading skirt swished around her. "I know it's stupid that our first day of school is on a Friday, but there's a party at Eric Nathan's house tonight. Are you going?"

"Yeah." Angie giggled. "No seniors from last year are around. They're all long gone."

"Yeah!" Marissa whooped. "We rule this school now. Hells yeah." She bobbed her head. Her ponytail swished up and down and she did a little cheering motion as she did. All in all, she caught the attention of every male in our vicinity.

"Hey, uh," I spoke up.

Both of their grins slid away and all attention was back on me.

I sighed. Was this how I wanted it? To take away their fun all the time? But I managed a smile and cleared my throat. "So I was wondering about Casey and her friends this year. I know they aren't too happy with us."

Marissa snorted. "Oh please. Let me handle her. It will be my pleasure, Alex. You just worry about being you, all perfect and beautiful. We mortals can only hope to be as perfect as you."

My eyes went wide. Was she kidding? "Are you serious?"

She just frowned and shrugged as she turned away.

I glanced at Angie. "You feel that way, too?"

Her eyes darted from me to Marissa before she let out a surrendering sigh. Her hands dropped to her sides still with her books, and she gave me a helpless grin. "What do you want me to say? You don't do anything intentionally, but you *are* kind of perfect. I get angry and lash out. Marissa screws around with guys and does your dirty work."

My mouth fell open. "I can't believe I'm hearing this."

Marissa rolled her eyes and looked back with a frustrated huff. "Oh come on, Alex. You don't say anything wrong. You don't do anything wrong. You always look gorgeous. I mean, look at you. You're tall and thin. You have a nice ass and boobs. Ethan was drop-dead gorgeous, and you're the female version of him, all dark eyes and full lips. I feel like you wake up and your skin naturally sparkles."

Angie barked out a laugh. "And here I thought she woke up in the morning and little birds helped do her hair."

They shared another look of amusement. "And mice run in her dress while the birds drop it over her. And everything fits perfectly as her horse puts his head through the door's window and has her hairbrush in his mouth."

They dissolved into laughter, but I could only stand there in shock. Really? That was how they thought of me? A disgruntled rumble started in my stomach, and I felt it rise up at an alarming rate. I was nauseous a second later and felt vomit in my throat. Did they not realize what they had lectured me on a month ago? But maybe they didn't remember it. Maybe they had forgotten how Jesse only had to snap his finger, and I was at his beck and call.

A shiver raced up my spine. He was gone. I wouldn't see him, I didn't know when or if I would see him again.

When the bell rang, Marissa and Angie stopped sharing Snow White jokes at my expense and sighed. Angie groaned. "God, here we go. First period, girls."

Marissa wiped at her eye and sniffed. "Yeah, we can do it. It's the beginning of our last year."

I looked at them as if they'd both lost their heads.

They rolled their eyes at my expression. Angie headed out first with a grin, "I'm off to college biology. See you two later."

Two other cheerleaders whisked Marissa away before either of us could reply, but as I watched them, I was happy for them. Justin held his arm out for Angie as she came to his side, and the two of them walked together down the hallway. On the other end of the hallway was Marissa. Half her friends seemed to bounce in excitement down the hallway while the other half, like her, seemed to strut. Guys turned and watched their group. From the hidden smirks and winks, Marissa's friends were fully aware of the power they had over the male population.

"Hi!"

I jumped out of my skin as I whirled around, patting my chest and trying to regain my breath when I realized it was just Eric. He had a small grin that matched the whites in his blue eyes, which were warm as he looked down at me.

"Hi."

"What class do you have?"

"I have a free period now."

"So . . ."

"So, probably the library. Why?"

"Oh." He bobbed his head in approval. "A bunch of us are headed to the cafeteria. It's way easier to work and stuff there, plus there's the vending machines. We can't snack in the library. Or talk. You wanna come? It'd be fun to talk."

"Talk?"

"Yeah. Talk. You know, see how your summer went and everything. I was looking for you at a bunch of the parties this last month, but I didn't see you. Were you sick?"

"Oh no." Jesse had been at those parties. "Nothing like that." I hadn't wanted to prolong the good-bye or worse, end up getting attached to sleeping in his bed.

"Oh. Okay." He scratched his head. When one of the football players shouted his name, he flashed them a grin. "Do you want to come? Chester was in Mississippi all summer, and I guess he's got some doozies for stories."

"Uh." I was lost. Did I want to talk? Did that stand for more? And then I shook my head at myself. I needed to relax. "Yeah. I'll come to talk."

His smile froze for a moment, but then he doubled its brightness. "Good. That's awesome. I'll buy you a soda even."

I laughed at myself. Oh dear. Look at me, so tense at getting a soda from someone. I was an idiot. "Thanks. I'll get the next time."

Eric laughed beside me as we turned for the cafeteria. "Sounds great. Think of it as a date." And he winked at me before he opened the door over my head and I passed under his arm.

As I went through, something flooded me. It felt good, relaxing. It felt right. My chest loosened a little bit. I could breathe easier. It lasted about a second. I watched in horror as Eric sat. He tossed his bag to one empty stool and hopped on the other one. As he rested his forearms on the table, his smile seemed contagious to the people across from him. One of them was Jesse's ex-girlfriend, Sarah Shastaine.

She gave Eric a shy smile and then tucked a strand of her soft blonde hair back. When he turned and motioned for me to join them, she turned as well. The same horror was in her eyes. I saw it for a split second before she turned away, but it was enough. Hurt, fear, longing, and another emotion all flashed over her face. My chest was so tight again.

Sarah Shastaine was perfect. Angie and Marissa might've given me grief about being perfect, but she was the real deal. She was petite with a heart shaped face. She was nice. She was popular. So many guys lined up to date her, and I'd heard one of them groan to his buddy that he wanted to scoop her up and shield her from the world. There was something fallen in her demeanor.

Had Jesse done that? Had he hurt her that much?

Had he broken her? Tears came to my eyes, but I held them at bay. Was he going to do the same to me? But that was preposterous. I hadn't seen him in a month. I didn't know the next time I would see him.

"Come on, Alex!" Eric gestured to me again. His smile seemed so genuine.

I was the worst person in the world.

As I sat, Sarah peeked up and gave me a cautious wave. "Hi, Alexandra."

"Sarah." My tone was equally as cautious. What was she going to say?

Then she cleared her throat. It was so soft and dainty sounding. All the bigger guys in the room positioned themselves toward our table. I knew they wanted to protect her still.

Her eyes were downcast as she played with her notebook. "How's Jesse doing?"

From the slight hitch in her tone, I knew she was still in love with him. I knew it. I was horrible. My voice came out raspy. "He's . . . okay."

She looked up. Her blue eyes were startlingly beautiful. They shimmered as they held mine captive. "Really?"

I jerked a shoulder up.

Another sad smile came from her before she dipped her head back down. "That's good."

I could hear the relief in her voice and cringed against it. She really still loved him.

"He deserves all the success that he's had recently."

I found myself nodding with her. "Yeah, you're right. He's doing really great."

Then she grinned at Eric. "And you're going to be as

successful as him. You'll lead our Wolverines to a state championship this year. I know it."

"Yeah." His grin slipped a bit and he leaned forward. The Adam's apple in his throat bobbed up and down. As he cleared his throat, he glanced down at the floor. "I'll sure try, I know that much."

"What does she mean?"

He shrugged. "Nothing much."

"Oh, that's not true." Sarah reached forward and placed her dainty hand over his. "He's the starting forward this year. And our captain."

"Really?"

He lifted another shoulder and looked away. "It doesn't mean much."

"It means a lot, Eric." Sarah disagreed with him. Her sparkling eyes wouldn't look away. "Jesse had big shoes for you to fill, but I have no doubt you're up for the job. You'll do wonderful."

He laughed, but the sound was uneasy.

I straightened in my seat and reassessed Jesse's perfect ex-girlfriend. Who was she kidding? I wasn't intending to be mean, but Eric couldn't fill Jesse's shoes on his best day. Jesse was going to go professional. Everyone knew that. Eric would be lucky if he got a scholarship at a lower level college. I might've checked out from a lot of school activities over the last year, but that was the truth. Even I knew it. For her to pump him up, make him feel as if he could do what Jesse could, told me a few things about Sarah Shastaine.

But I bit my lip.

Eric seemed uncomfortable, and he kept glancing at me. When I gave him a small smile, he relaxed, but his shoulders still drooped. I turned to Sarah. Her smile was still dazzling and the warmth in her eyes didn't shift away.

It really only occurred to me right then that she believed what she just said and didn't see one ounce of harm in it.

As she glanced at me one more time, I took a second to try to see what was under her surface. I had always thought of Sarah as an angel, but now I wasn't so sure. Then again, I had never asked why Jesse had suddenly ended his thing with her. I always figured it was because of Ethan. It had been the same time he had stopped staying at our house and the beginning of when he turned from nice guy into cold-hearted player last year.

Maybe there was another reason.

6

Two months went by quicker than I realized. Angie and I went to every football game. Justin played and Marissa cheered, so we supported both of them. I never told either of them of that weird day with Sarah in the cafeteria. We didn't interact much after that. We had one class together, and she was always partners with her two friends in the class. Eric was in the same class, but he always ended up in my group. And I thought about Jesse every day.

I tried not to. I really did, but I couldn't help it.

The few times that my father was at home, he always had ESPN on in the background. And most of those times, there seemed to be a discussion about upcoming freshman that would be watched for the season. Jesse's name was never left out. And then there was the time my mom had an entertainment gossip show on the television. Jesse's dad had a movie premiere on the red carpet. The cameras always talked about Malcolm Hunt with a snapshot to Jesse, the future star basketball son of his.

That premiere turned into too many, along with all the other media interviews. It wasn't customary to pay attention to the producer's son, but when that son looked like Jesse

Hunt and already had the reputation he did, most of them included his name in the interviews. And the same video footage of the time Jesse attended a premiere would roll. He'd been dressed in a black tuxedo with his hair still buzzed and the same unemotional look he'd had during his senior year. At least he hadn't taken a date. I breathed easier when I saw he was solo, but then I told myself it didn't mean a thing.

He never called. He hadn't visited. There'd been no communication from him and I knew there wouldn't be.

So, when Homecoming rolled around at the end of October, I accepted Eric's invitation to be his date, even though I wasn't sure I should've. He didn't seem to notice my reluctance or the guilt I carried after. He was all smiles every time he saw me in class and was eager to plan the details of the date.

"Hey, you." Angie's dressed swished around her as she carried it with one hand. She grimaced when she came into my bedroom and pouted at the sight of my bed. "We haven't even gotten to the game and I already just want to fall asleep."

"Look at you. You're beautiful."

She was, in a princess-style green dress with taffeta underneath. It wasn't Angie, but she said Justin picked it out. She aimed to please, and that dress was going to please him. Her hair was her style. She had it piled high in a braid, intertwined with flowers. She always said she wanted it pretty, but simple and out of the way. It was that indeed.

She groaned as she turned my fan on and stood in front of it. "I don't know about that, but I'm damn jealous right now. You're lucky you didn't make Homecoming Court, otherwise you'd be wearing that gorgeous pink thing you've got in your closet instead of waiting until the last second to put it on. Oh no, you would be sweating your ass off right now, even though you know you're going to be freezing it off at the game tonight." A huff emitted from her throat as she cursed and sat on my bed. "I don't give a rat's ass if my dress is messed up. This thing looks ridiculous on me."

I chuckled and turned back to the mirror to finish my makeup. It wasn't much, some eyeliner and lipstick. I was done two seconds later. "You're being a good girlfriend, that's what you're doing. And since you don't really care about Homecoming and Justin does, you're doing the right thing in my mind."

"Mine, too." She groaned. "But, hell, I'm suffering here. He doesn't have to put on his tuxedo until after the game. He only has to show up on my arm at halftime. It sucks being a girl."

"I agree with that."

Then she sighed. "Have you heard what Marissa's plans are?"

When she struggled to stand, I caught her hand in mine and pulled her upright. Then I shook my head. "I don't think she's going to cheer tonight and change, just change into her dress in the locker room. That's all I know."

"I'd still like to know how she got Cord Tatum to come back to school as her Homecoming date. She's got some balls for that one. I didn't think any alumni returned to high school, especially if they went to Grant West and ran in the same circles as Jesse Hunt." Angie laughed when she gathered her dress up once more to fit through my doorway again.

I stopped at her words and a shiver passed through me. She talked about him as if he weren't a real person anymore. As she continued to muse about Marissa's powers over the opposite sex, I realized that maybe Jesse had become nonexistent to her. He'd never interacted with her. He had only been another member on Justin's sports team, whichever it was at the time.

When she continued down the hallway and down the stairs, I knew she hadn't looked back.

I was still rooted in my bedroom. I hadn't forgotten that Cord would be going to the dance with us, and I hadn't forgotten that he was friends with Jesse, but I hadn't dwelled on it, either. I couldn't stop thinking about it and the idea of it, and it made my stomach twist. I would be in the presence of someone who saw Jesse on a daily basis, and the thought had me sweating.

I turned the fan on myself and counted from fifty to one.

I wasn't going to see Jesse. This was ridiculous. What was wrong with me?

"Hey, get your cute butt down here. I want to get this night started so it'll end faster. Hurry up!"

When I went downstairs, I never stopped to look in the kitchen or living room. If anyone was in there, they didn't care. I didn't even think they were aware it was October.

When we got to the game, Angie waved and went one way. I went the other.

"Alex! Over here! Over here!" Ben pumped his hand back and forth in the air as he yelled over the crowd. He pointed to the seat beside him. "I have a seat for you! Over here!"

Some guys yelled at him to shut up, but my coworker beamed at me. He was dressed in our school's colors: yellow and black. He wore a yellow hat, a yellow scarf, yellow gloves, and he even waved a yellow hankie in the air. His coat was black.

As I went through the crowd to his side, he clapped his hands from excitement. "Hey! I'm vibrating with giddiness tonight."

"Why?" I brushed back my hair and tried to peer around the three guys in front of us.

"It's *Homecoming*." He spoke as if it were the next up-and-coming event that was going to change our lives. "Do you have a date? Wait. I heard that Eric Nathan asked you." He nudged me with his elbow and winked. "Where is he? Why isn't he sitting with you?"

I laughed and elbowed him back. "Because he's on the Homecoming Court. They wait somewhere else."

"Oh. Wait. You're his date. Don't you have to go out there with him?"

"They paired him up with a girl who's already in the court. I don't have to put my dress on until the dance."

"Oh." He sounded disappointed.

"You okay with that?"

"Yeah, whatever." Ben sniffled and jerked forward.

"Ben."

"What?" He didn't look at me.

"Ben."

"What?" He still didn't look.

I sighed. "Are you going to the dance with anybody?"

"No," he clipped out. His bottom lip was thrust out in a pout. "But, that's okay. It's not like it means anything to me. It's not like I'm a senior too, and I have other friends that I could've gone with."

My eyes closed. He did have other friends. He had two others, but they were younger. Ben might've been my coworker and someone who cared about me, but he was seen as an outcast to everybody else. I was the insensitive one who didn't look at things from his perspective.

"I'm sorry. Would you go with me and Eric?"

He turned in a flash, his smile blinding me. "Really?"

"Really."

"Oh, thank you! Thank you!" He bundled me to him in a big hug and rocked me back and forth. "You're so great."

"Hey." Someone cleared their throat behind me, and I turned around. The smile died and the laughter faded away. Cord Tatum stood at the end of our aisle in a black leather bomber jacket and custom-fitted jeans. He had jet-black hair with the ends sticking straight up and dark brown eyes to match.

Almost out of instinct, I knew this guy was Marissa's counterpart. She had met her match with him. I knew he had been part of Ethan's class, but I couldn't remember what he had been like in high school. I did know that he went to Grant West and was on the same team as Jesse. Two basketball stars from the same school was a big thing around our town.

"Marissa told me I could sit with you." He held his hand out. "I'm Cord. I don't know if you remember me or not."

"Hi. Alex Connors."

I shook his hand. It was firm and steady. He squeezed my hand before he lifted a hand in a wave to Ben. "Hi, I'm Cord."

"Ben." His voice came out as a squeak. He seemed mortified and squeaked again as he huddled beside me.

As Cord sat beside me, he pulled out some leather gloves and slipped them on. He shuddered in his jacket. "Man, its cold out here. It's a little bit warmer at Grant West, by ten degrees at least. I forget how much that makes a difference." He laughed a little. "I haven't been back home since last Christmas. I think my mom had a heart attack when I walked through the door. All her biscuits went on the floor except the one that's stuck to the ceiling."

He talked to me as if we were best friends. Was he like this with everyone or had Marissa spoken so much about me he felt like he knew me? My tongue felt heavy as I asked, "So how did you and Marissa get together?"

"Through Jesse." He grinned and caught my gaze. His eyes were so warm.

My heart stopped. Through Jesse?

"Really?" My throat felt constricted now. "How did that happen?"

He laughed again and hunched his shoulders forward for warmth. "She kept calling the house one night. Jesse was tired of it so he told me to talk to her."

"She was calling him?"

He nodded and gave me another good-natured grin. "Yep. I told her off. She told me off right back, and then I started to take her calls when she would call." He laughed again. "Man, I can't believe how many girls throw themselves at Jesse. He's a big deal around here, huh?"

"You could say that."

My heart sank at his words. Marissa had still chased him. When I felt tears coming to my eyes, I stood up. "Excuse me. I'm going to get something to drink."

"Alex, get me one, too!" Ben hollered, but I hurried down the bleachers and through the crowd. More and more people stood between me and some fresh air. I needed that air. I needed that freedom. Everything was suffocating me.

As I slipped around a building, I heaved in deep breaths. No one else was there. Thankful for the privacy, I pressed my forehead against the building and took more breaths.

How could she do that? Didn't she remember?

Betrayal, longing, and hurt settled over me.

How was I going to last the night? Oh God. Was I going to say anything to Angie about it?

"Alex?"

I stiffened. Eric had the worst timing.

He came farther around the side of the building, a frown on his face. "Are you okay? What's wrong?"

"Nothing." I tried to smile as continued to try to catch my breath and slow my heartbeat. "I'm fine. What are you doing?"

His frown doubled. "I saw you leave the stands and thought something was wrong. Are you sure you're okay?"

"I'm fine." My best friend stabbed me in the back. "Really. You look really handsome." I nodded to the tuxedo he had on under his jacket.

"Oh." He shrugged. "Yeah. Not as beautiful as you'll be tonight, or that you already are. You already are beautiful. You're always beautiful, actually. Even in school, and I'm going to stop talking." He gave me a sheepish look. "You sure you're okay? You can talk to me, you know. You can talk to me about anything."

I held my breath and blinked back the tears that threatened. He seemed like such a nice guy and I was upset about another guy. What was wrong with me?

"You're a really nice guy." I sighed.

His smile slipped a little. "Ah, the words of death."

"What?"

He looked down at the ground. "No guy wants to be the nice guy. Nice guys finish last."

My heart broke again. What was I doing? Here was a great guy and I was waiting for another one who broke me every time. I gave Jesse my virginity and look what I had for it? Nothing. He was away. I was here. He couldn't even bring himself to call me. Yet, here Eric was, proclaiming how beautiful he thought I was.

I was such an idiot.

I reached out before I knew what I was doing. When my hand touched his, his head whipped up, and his eyes went wide. He grasped my hand tight and pulled me close. His arms lifted and he hugged me. That was it, nothing more. I let out a surrendering breath and let myself enjoy what he was offering. Nothing. He was offering a hug.

It'd been a long time since I'd only been held. It felt needed.

I hugged him back.

Eric hugged me tighter to him, but then he stepped back and ran a hand through his hair. "Uh, I don't really know how to say this, so I guess I'm just going to say it." He took a deep breath. "Okay, here it goes." His eyes found mine. They were piercing. "I want to be more than friends, Alex. I really like you. I've really liked you for a while, but you seemed so lost last year. I, uh, would you consider going on a real date with me? Tonight doesn't have to be it, just some other night."

I stood there. I had no thoughts.

He kicked at the ground and pushed his hands in his jacket's pockets. Then he glanced around. "You can think about it. You don't have to answer right now. We could go bowling or eat or go see a movie or whatever." His shoulders lifted up and down again. "Let me know, you know?"

"I will."

"Really?"

"I'll let you know."

"Oh."

Someone yelled his name, and he gave me resigned look. "I guess that's my call. Are you coming to watch the court?"

I nodded. "Yeah, I'm coming."

"Okay." He jerked forward and pressed his lips against my forehead in a hurried kiss. "Sorry. I—sorry. Okay. See you later."

He waved again before he disappeared around the building, and I was left alone once more. I was such a moron. Then I took a deep breath. I stopped thinking. I stopped feeling. As I went back to the game, I knew everything would sort itself out.

It had to.

7

A ngie collapsed in a chair beside me and groaned as she kneaded her calves. "My feet and calves are so damn stiff from these heels. Tell me how much I love Justin."

"You love Justin so much that you're wearing that ridiculous dress for him."

She grunted and leaned back. "Yeah, and a part of me thinks he chose this dress to make me squirm. I swear, he's paid more attention to Marissa's black little bitty than this poof of his dream. Ugh. Boys drive me crazy."

I suppressed my instant frown. I hadn't told her about Marissa, and I wasn't sure if I really wanted to. She'd get mad. She'd probably throw a drink on her, and then my two best friends would be at odds again. I had no idea what to do.

What Marissa did had hurt me, but I didn't know the whole story. She might've been calling him about me. Cord could've gotten it all wrong, so I had made the decision to ask Marissa on my own, and not at the dance.

"I still want to know how the hell she got Cord to come back for a dance. I didn't even think she knew him." She narrowed her eyes as she nursed her drink. "Do you know?"

I froze.

"You do know."

I refused to look over. I couldn't meet her eyes. She'd see there was something wrong.

"Alex." Angie scooted her chair closer. "Come on, tell me. I know you know. You do this weird statue thing when you've been caught at something. Just tell me. I won't say anything. Is it dirty? Did they do the deed when he was a senior? That's it, isn't it? I knew Marissa had slept with more guys than just Gavin that year, but nooo, she swears she was only with him that year." She snorted and slapped a hand on the table. "She's such a little slut."

I held my breath and counted to twenty. I had to because I wanted to spill. It took every ounce of my control to keep my lips shut. I owed it to Marissa to let her explain, and I owed myself to find out if my best friend had really gone behind my back for some guy.

Angie chuckled and finished her drink. "And I mean that in a good way. Only that girl could get three guys wrapped around her finger at one dance."

"Yeah." I sighed and then looked at my lap. Everything was burning inside me to tell Angie, but I couldn't. I had to stop with this debate.

"Hey, so, how's it going with Eric tonight? He seems nice."

A different tension filled me and I froze again.

"Uh oh." Angie put her glass down and scooted so close to me that her leg pressed against mine. "Tell me whatever it is. I'm your best friend. It's a sin for you not to tell me, so spill the beans, woman."

The words spilled from my lips. "He asked me out. He said he likes me more than friends and he wants to go out on a date with me." I almost went into my dilemma about Jesse, but I hadn't spoken about him for almost three months. It was fair if they had forgotten about him, but then I felt a pang of conscience. Was that what happened with Marissa? Had she forgotten what he was to me?

"Oooh!" Angie squealed. "Are you going to go out with him? You have to. He's such a nice guy. Come on, Alex!"

"I don't know."

"You have to. Trust me, if you don't, he's going to be scooped up by someone else. Eric is really popular. There are a lot of girls who would kill to be in your shoes. What's the hang up?"

I hesitated. She wouldn't like hearing what I had to say.

Then she sighed in disgust and scooted away. "Oh, my God. Really? Do *not* say Jesse's name. Please do not say his name."

I shrugged.

"OH! Alex!" She hit herself in the forehead with her hand. "I can't believe you. I'm not saying this to be mean, but he's long gone. He's at Grant West. He is in a different lifestyle now. He's hanging out with the Hollywood people for crying out loud. I watch television, too."

I smoothed out my dress and tried not to squirm under her intense gaze. I didn't believe for one second that Jesse was hanging out with the Hollywood crowd. I believed that he went as a favor to his dad, but I also believed that he hadn't gone since. Jesse hated his dad. That wasn't known by anyone else except my family and his, but Angie said some truth. He was long gone, and he made it apparent that he had no interest in coming back anytime soon.

I sighed and sat there, wondering why I hadn't jumped at the chance to date Eric Nathan. He was normal. He was there, and he thought I was beautiful.

"Hey!" Marissa chirped as she and Cord took their seats across from us at the table. Ben dropped in his and grabbed some napkins to wipe his forehead. His panting had turned into wheezing. "Where's Eric?'

Cord tapped her shoulder and pointed across the gym.

"Why is he talking to Casey Wright?"

Angie tapped my leg. "See."

"See what?" Marissa looked between us. Her eyes were lit with anticipation. "See what? Fill me in."

I was about to tell her that it was nothing, but Angie rushed out, "Eric asked her out."

Marissa gasped. She clapped her hands to her cheeks and squealed in her seat. "Oh, my God. That's so exciting. Alex, say something. Aren't you happy about that?"

"Uh, yeah, I guess."

"You're not excited about that?" She watched me closely and frowned. "Are you waiting for—"

"Have you talked to him recently?" I hadn't wanted to ask, but putting her on the spot was better than the alternative. She didn't answer, though. She just sat and started at me with wide eyes.

"What are you girls talking about?" Cord asked as he lounged back with his arm thrown over Marissa's chair. He pulled his tuxedo collar out and exchanged a look with Ben.

"Nothing," Marissa said quickly.

Angie frowned at her.

"So . . . have you talked to him recently?"

"Why would she have talked to him? He's your—"

"Yes." She shoved back her chair and stood up. Her hands held on to the table. "I called him after he left. I have no excuse for that."

I shoved my chair back as well. My heart was starting to pick up its pace and my cheeks were warm. "What did you promise him? What were you after? Were you going to drive there if he said yes?"

Angie's eyes had widened, and she was white in the face. She stood with us but held on to her drink with a death grip.

"Alex, I'm sorry—"

"Sorry for what? What'd you do?" I needed her to say it. I needed to hear the words.

"For . . ." She closed her eyes and took a deep breath. "For—what do you want me to say?"

"The *truth*." It ripped out of me.

She gulped. The blood drained from her face. As she started to sway on her feet, Cord jumped up and caught her elbow. "Hey, whoa. Hey. You okay?" He frowned at us and then shook his head. "I think maybe we should call it a night. There's stuff going on between you three, but I don't think it's worth Marissa getting sick."

Angie snorted. Her hand found her hip and she stuck it out.

Marissa swayed more unsteadily on her feet. She was still holding on to the table, and her knuckles had grown white.

"Okay." Cord shot us another dark look as he drew Marissa against him. He pressed a kiss to her forehead and then draped his coat around her shoulders. "Let's head home, huh?"

She nodded and let him lead her away.

Angie glared after them. She threw back the rest of her punch and then ground up her cup into a plastic ball. When it fell from her hand, she snorted in disgust. "I can't believe her. Really, I can't believe her. She knew about you and him. Hell, she knew before when she was trying to go at him. Is she mentally screwed up, or what? Is it her ego? Does she really have to conquer *every guy* out there?"

Justin came up to the table at that moment. He took one look at Angie and spun around on his heel.

She watched him leave. "That's probably for the best. I'd unleash my anger on him and that's all sorts of wrong." She sighed and looked at me. "Are you okay?"

"Whatever. I'll deal." But that wasn't the truth. The truth was that it stung, a lot. Tears threatened to fall, and I swallowed a lump down my throat. I couldn't dwell on it. That would make me think of what she'd done and inevitably that would make me think of Jesse. I was really trying to stop thinking about him.

"Hey." Eric approached with two glasses in his hands. He handed one to me. "Justin said something was wrong."

Angie gave him a "duh" look. "And I bet he warned you to stay away."

Eric stiffened. His eyes skirted from her to me before he gave us both a sheepish look. "Uh, yeah, but I didn't. Was that not the right thing to do?"

"No." Angie's hands found her hips, and she turned to scan the room. "You're doing the right thing. Where's my boyfriend? I've got something different to unleash on him."

I couldn't hold back a grin as she winked at me when she headed out. Those two would be long gone within minutes, so I glanced at Ben.

His eyes looked ready to pop out but he was still in his chair. Beads of sweat had formed on his forehead. He lifted a handkerchief to wipe them away. I knew he'd been sweating since we got into the gym. With all the hot bodies and dancing, it was on the verge of a sauna.

"Did you have fun?"

He nodded, still speechless.

I chuckled. My hand slipped into Eric's. "I think it's time we call it a night."

Eric grasped my hand. A smile lit up his face.

Ben jerked his head in a nod. His second chin wobbled from the movement and then he struggled to his feet. "Bye. See you at work tomorrow morning."

We watched him go. No one said good-bye to him and he collected his coat in silence.

My heart ached for him. In some ways, I felt like my life was similar to Ben's, but in others I knew I was lucky to still have Angie as my friend.

Eric watched beside me. "He's a nice guy. Junior, right?"

"He's a senior with us."

"He is? I don't remember him in any of our classes."

That was Ben's problem. He was always there but in the background. Before I started getting sad again, I whirled around with a bright smile. I slipped both of my arms around Eric's waist underneath his tuxedo coat. "Are you hungry?"

Eric's eyes darkened. His smile softened as he stared down at me. "Starving."

"Me, too."

My heart skipped a beat. We stared at each other for a second, and I didn't think either of us breathed. The moment was suspended in time. I didn't know what it was or what it meant, but it felt right. I felt that everything would be okay right then, and I wanted to keep feeling like that.

"Come on." Eric's voice dropped to a husky murmur, and he led me outside with his hand in mine. As I waited by the door, he went back for our coats.

"Here you go." But he was back already.

My arms went behind me and he slid my coat over them. He rounded and pulled it the rest of the way, making sure that I would be warm enough when we walked outside. He tucked all the corners in the right spot before he pulled me close for another hug.

It was delicious.

I closed my eyes and burrowed my head against his shoulder. He brushed back some strands of my hair. The feel of his fingers against my skin gave me a loving feeling. He touched me tenderly, so softly that I could feel the yearning from him. Or maybe that was me. Did I yearn for his touch? I never had before, but as I moved away a step and held his gaze, I was cold.

He chuckled as he took my hand again. "Come on. I thought you said you were hungry."

"I am."

"What do you think? Burgers? Tacos?"

"A big fat cheeseburger, please." I felt giddy in that moment. I was breaking some rule that I didn't know yet.

"Sounds perfect." Eric's smile softened again. He pulled me close and placed his arm around my shoulders as we walked to his truck. The cold air blasted me, pulling me from the fairy tale reverie I'd been in. When he helped me inside and rounded the truck for his door, I paused. What were we doing?

But then he was inside, and it wasn't long before the heat warmed me and dulled my thoughts once again.

Eric was a gentleman as he drove to a fast food place and ordered us both big and juicy cheeseburgers. We shared a large fry between us. When he took me home, I experienced bittersweet emotions. I was content and satiated, but I was empty and starving at the same time. I just wasn't sure for what or whom. I didn't want to think of those questions any longer.

For once, I turned my thoughts off and just basked in the warmth Eric showered on me.

When he parked outside of my home, we could tell the television was on in my living room.

"Did your parents wait up for you?" Eric frowned at me. He narrowed his eyes in concern. "I could've brought you back earlier. Are you in trouble?"

I almost snorted at that question. "No. I'm fine. I'm sure it's either my dad or mom. Sometimes they have trouble sleeping." I laughed then. "I don't even think they realized tonight was Homecoming."

"Are you serious?"

I waved away the concern. "Don't worry about it. My parents are in their own world right now." My hand slipped into his. I squeezed once. "I'm sure it's hard for a parent to lose a child. They'll snap out of it one of these days."

Eric frowned but didn't respond.

In all honesty, if someone had told me that same thing, I would be at a loss for words. So I shrugged again and forced a happy note in my voice. "Don't worry. My dad won't come out here with a stern warning or anything."

He still frowned. "Are you sure?"

"I am." I reached forward for a hug, and because I didn't want him to worry, I pressed a quick kiss to his cheek. "Thanks, Eric." And then I hurried out of his truck and inside. My heart was pounding. I wasn't ready for a kiss on the lips, but I knew he'd been distracted. He had sucked in his breath, his body stiffened, and I felt his hand start to curve around my waist before I slipped away.

I sighed and leaned against my door.

I could hear the sports channel in the living room, so I knew my dad was there. As I stopped in the doorway, I saw that he was asleep on the couch with a blanket at his feet.

Pain speared through me, but I pushed it down.

I held the bottom of my dress in one hand so the swishing sound wouldn't wake him and gently pulled the blanket to cover him. As his chest rose up and down, his forehead crinkled in a sleeping kind of worry.

I didn't wait around to see if he'd wake up. And I didn't wait around to see if he was dreaming of Ethan. I did, so it made sense if my parents did as well. With my heart heavier, I tiptoed up to my room. The moonlight streamed through my window, so I didn't turn on the lights as I slipped out of my dress and changed into pajama shorts and a tank. After I went to the bathroom and washed up for bed, I returned and closed the door behind me again.

I flicked on the lights that hung over my closet.

When I looked over, Jesse was on the edge of my bed. He lifted the corner of his lip. "Fun night?"

My heart stopped.

The moonlight filtered over him. His high cheekbones were illuminated from the light, along with the curve of his lips. As he stood, I could see that he'd gotten leaner, but when he drew closer to me, I knew he was also stronger.

I wet my lips. My legs started to tremble.

Then he was in front of me, within touching distance, and I could only look at his chest. His tee shirt looked soft to the touch, and I ached to feel it. I ached for him. Oh God.

He smelled delicious. He was so close. His jeans touched the thin material of my pajama shorts. They rubbed against me before his hand lifted for my waist. As it touched me, I jumped backward.

My throat was thick now, but I choked out, "What are you doing here?"

He bent forward. I felt his breathing against my forehead, and then his lips touched me softly. One of his hands lifted and skimmed a gentle finger down the side of my face. He trailed it to my chin and tilted my face up to meet his gaze.

I felt a swift kick inside my stomach. It was aimed low and delivered with perfection. I didn't know if I would recover from it.

"I wanted to see you."

"Why?"

His hand cupped the side of my face, and he angled it so he looked straight down at me. His eyes were dark. A molten desire was there, but blanketed. I felt it reach for me, and everything I had decided that evening melted away. His thumb started to rub back and forth over my cheek. I closed my eyes and leaned closer. I needed him.

His lips touched beside my eye, then the corner of my lips. He paused.

I gasped.

My heart raced now, and I surged closer to him.

His lips touched mine.

Finally.

Then he whispered, "Your parents?"

I shook my head, but I pulled away to lock the door. After that, he tugged me down to the bed, and it wasn't long before we were naked and connected once again.

When he pushed inside, I let myself go. It might've been

wrong, but I felt like it was right. And then he started thrusting. My hips moved to match, and I stopped thinking. I could only feel. Jesse groaned in my ear, and I turned to meet his lips. When I captured them, we groaned together.

I wasn't sure how long we lay in bed afterward. I felt replete, and he had collapsed on top of me. His head rested on my chest, and I stroked his hair. I could've stayed there forever. With the cold wind against my window and the small clear lights around my closet, my room had a romantic feel to it. It was our corner away from the world.

When his phone lit up from the floor, both of us cursed.

Jesse grinned at me before he rolled over to check it. Then he cursed again as he sat up. "I have to go."

"You just got here."

He grimaced as he read more of his text. "Cord got arrested."

"What?"

He shrugged. "I don't know what happened. I gotta go and bail him out."

"You're joking."

"I'm not." He stood from the bed and started looking for his clothes. As a big yawn came over him, he shook his head and ran a hand over his face. "I've gotta wake up. I thought I'd be in bed with you all night."

I scooted up against the headboard and gathered my comforter around me, hugging it over my breasts. I felt helpless. He had to go. That was the deal. I wanted him to stay, and had to force myself not to ask if he would be coming back. No good would come from that answer.

So I heaved a deep breath. "Someone asked me out tonight."

Jesse stopped what he was doing. The shirt he'd been about to pull over his head fell to the side and he sat at the end of the bed. His voice was low. "Who?"

"Eric Nathan."

"Oh."

What did that mean? Did it mean anything at all? My chest was tight as I asked, "What are you thinking?"

He snorted and pulled his shirt over his head. His movements were rough as he bent to jerk his shoes on.

"Jesse?"

He snapped, "What's your problem? We screw. That's all we do. I don't give a shit if you're dating my replacement."

"Your replacement?"

He started for the door, but I hurried and got there first. I pressed my back against it and held the handle tightly behind me.

He stopped an inch from me but stared past my shoulders. He refused to meet my gaze. He clipped out, "Let me leave."

"What do you mean replacement?"

His hand ran over his head and he seemed to seethe. "Come on. Let me leave."

My heart was pounding. When wasn't it? And then I gulped. It was calm whenever I was in his arms. I almost groaned at that thought but rasped out, "Jesse, you don't mean for me? Do you?"

He chuckled and shook his head. Arrogance came over him. "Nah, Alex. I meant in basketball. He was second string forward, my alternate. The dipshit never played a game last year. He's going to tank this year." The smirk grew ugly. "Now I'm glad I ruined that sport for him. He can't touch my records. I'd love for him to try. And everyone's going to hope he'll lead them to state champs. When he won't, they'll hate him. I couldn't have planned that better."

My heart sank. Of course he hadn't meant for me.

He reached around me, and this time, I didn't give him a fight. I was shifted to the side and he slipped through. When the door was going to slide to a quiet close, his hand stopped it and he poked his head around the door. "Don't let him screw you."

Before I could ask what *exactly* he meant by that, he was gone. I went to the window. It wasn't long before I saw him dart past my window and hurry to the Ferrari parked in front of the neighbor's house. He'd left through the back door, which meant my parents hadn't known he was there. I shouldn't have been surprised. They would've torn the door down if they had known. He was the closest reminder of Ethan. No matter how far they slipped into their numbed and dazed states, I knew they'd snap out of them for him. My parents loved Jesse more than they loved me.

It was something I learned after the funeral, and I had come to terms with it, even understood it. Hell. *I* loved Jesse more than myself. I couldn't blame my parents at all.

8

I stayed in the next day. Angie came over at one point to rant about the meaning of friendship, but she didn't last long. After an hour, she started checking her phone and glancing at the door. I knew she was itching to leave. Both of my friends had stopped visiting since Ethan's death, and I didn't blame them. There was an empty feeling in my home. I had grown used to it and was now almost comforted by it. I knew that was sad and twisted, but it was beyond my control.

After she left, I huddled under my covers and stayed there. One movie turned into two, which turned into three, and after the fourth, my stomach growled so loudly that I was forced to leave for the kitchen. Once I was down there, I stopped in the foyer.

There was no sound in the living room.

I circled through the first floor of our little house. Every room was empty. The basement was the same, and then, my heart starting to pound, I went upstairs. The bathroom was empty. My parents' master bedroom was empty. The room Jesse always used was empty as well, and the last room was Ethan's. His door was closed. It had been over a year now. My hand started to tremble, but I pushed open the door.

His black comforter was pulled straight over his bed. His pillows were piled high, along with the bag he had left on his bed that last day.

I drew in a shuddering breath.

It'd been a little over a year. I couldn't believe it.

After entering the room, I shut the door again and backed up to the wall.

I hadn't come into his room since his funeral, and I couldn't make myself look around it. His presence was so overwhelming; I felt as if he was in here, maybe on his bed, and he had looked up at my arrival. He always did that when I'd push open the door for some question or a stupid excuse to see if Jesse was with him. Some days, he'd tell me to leave, but other days he'd welcome my arrival.

I gasped out loud and tried to draw in another breath.

Then the tears started. Why did I feel him? Why did it seem as if he were right next to me? Then the hairs on the back of my neck stood straight up.

I had to get out of there.

I shot to my feet and sprinted down the hallway. I grabbed my purse, my coat, and I was out the door within moments.

I still felt him.

As I got into my car, my fingers were clumsy, and I dropped the keys twice. After the third time, I gritted my teeth and forced my hand to stop shaking enough for me to get them in the ignition. And then my phone went off. I jumped and gasped again. My eyes grew blurry as I reached for it. When I read Marissa's name on the screen, I sighed from relief.

Slowly, the world returned to focus and my heart stopped pounding in my ear. I was able to see once more.

As I hit the answer button, I collapsed back against my seat and sighed, "Yeah?"

"Oh my gosh." Marissa drew in her own breath. "Thank God you answered me. I've been calling you all night. I'm so, so, so sorry about Jesse. I really am."

"What happened to Cord last night?" I didn't want to hear anything she had to say about Jesse.

"Wait, what? What are you talking about?"

There was my answer. "Nothing. Never mind."

"Wait, did something happen to Cord last night? He dropped me off and was going to pick me up later. I was supposed to sneak out since my parents have become whack crazy with me lately, but he never showed. Did something happen? I assumed he ditched." Her voice raised a note. "Oh, my gosh. What if something did happen? I'm so horrible. I was cursing at him all night, and I even unfriended him on Facebook."

I regretted saying anything now.

"Alex, did something happen? Please tell me what you know. You know something, otherwise you wouldn't have asked about him. What happened? Please, please, please don't make this about you and me. I messed up. I am a horrible, horrible friend. I never should've called Jesse, but if I hadn't, I wouldn't have fallen in love with Cord. Please tell me!"

I sat back up again. My voice was quiet. "You love him?"

"Yes!" she cried out. "I didn't realize it until last night, and it was the most bittersweet night for me. I knew I might've lost you as a friend, but I realized that I loved Cord, and then I thought he ditched me, you know the rest. Please, *tell me!*"

I shook my head. I could already hear Angie's protests, but I tuned them out. "He was arrested."

"What? How? What happened?"

"I don't know. That's all I know."

"Alex," she pleaded.

"That's really all I know."

"Wait, how do you even know that? Cord was going to see

some of his old friends. Do you know Jeremy Benson and James Mazel? They graduated two years ahead of us."

"No, I don't know them." But I knew of them. They were the gods of the school before Jesse firmly took that reign over last year. I should've remembered they were friends with Cord. But I also remembered they were known to break a law or two.

My heart shuttered. I didn't want Jesse mixed up with them.

"I have to go, Marissa."

"What? Wait! What?"

But I hung up over her pleads and turned my car onto the road. My life might've been frozen at a standstill over the last year, but I wasn't going to let Jesse let his go down the drain. He might've been an ass at times, but he was a gifted ass, and he was meant for better things than the rest of us. I felt that in my bones.

My palms were sweaty as I drove to Jesse's house. And I felt ready to vomit at any moment. Everything in me was queasy and quivering. I took a deep breath as I pulled into their driveway. When I got outside, I smoothed my hands down my clothes. It was then that I cursed at myself. I was still dressed in my pajama pants and sweatshirt.

Good one, Alex.

I made a note to pack an extra bag of clothes for the next time I felt haunted by Ethan's presence.

And then I knew I had to stop stalling, so I marched up the front steps and rang the doorbell. Like the last time, Mary answered the door, but unlike the last time, she shook her head at me. "Not here, Miss Alex. He not here. He here." And she shoved a piece of paper in my hand.

I looked down and saw an address scribbled on it. When I looked back up to ask more questions, the door had already been closed.

Well, then.

I climbed back in my car and plugged the address into my phone's GPS. Thirty minutes later, I pulled up to a large brick home. Every window had light shining from it and I heard male voices and bass music as I got out of my car.

"Alex?"

I turned. Marissa was at the end of the driveway. She frowned at me as she pulled at the end of her hair with a hand.

She always did that when she was nervous.

"Hey." I crossed the street to her. "Whose house is this?"

"Jeremy Benson's." Disgust flared over her face. "I can't believe Cord is friends with him. He's become a loser. All he does is work at his dad's company and hang out at The Pub every night."

"Cord's in there?"

She sighed and dropped her hand from her hair. "I'm really sorry, Alex. I really am. I was just stupid and insecure. I kept calling Jesse like a stalker. I think a part of me hated the idea that you could get a guy I couldn't, and I know, I know. That makes me sound like scum. I am scum. I am. I will do anything to make it up to you. I swear!"

She stopped and held her breath.

I didn't say anything.

Then her head dropped. "And can you believe the worst part of it? I got his number from your phone." A pathetic giggle escaped her lips. "He doesn't even give his number out anymore, but I knew you had it. That's how sad I've become as a friend."

I didn't know if it was the tear she wiped away or the hitch in her voice, but I crumbled. I wasn't one to hold grudges, but I knew I had let her back in. "Stop blubbering. I get it."

"Really?" She wiped a second tear again as her face lit up.

I nodded. I wasn't going to hug her or anything, but I knew we'd be okay again.

"Oh, thank God," she breathed out in relief. "I was so scared that you were going to do the distance thing to me. I've seen you do it, and it scares the hell out of me."

"Distance thing?"

She nodded and wiped a third tear that slipped down her

cheek away. "Uh huh. You don't ever get mad at people, but you freeze them out. Once you put up a wall, you don't take it down. I was so scared that you were going to do that to me."

"That makes me sound horrible."

"Oh, no, Alex. Please, no. I don't want you to think that. It's just you." A sudden understanding came over her.

I backed away. I didn't want her to understand me. I didn't want anyone to understand me.

Her eyes widened, but then her arms dropped to her sides, and she forced a bright smile on. "Okay. So, are you going in there with me? I came over to make sure Cord was okay and chew him out for not calling me. I called Amanda Sherman. Her mom works at the station and she was there waiting for her to get off work last night. She said that she saw Jeremy and James Hazel get arrested, too."

"Oh."

"Wait, why are you here?" Her eyes narrowed. "You didn't come to chew Cord out for me?"

I bit the inside of my lip. I could've taken that, but I knew she'd see him anyway. I shook my head. "No. I came because of—"

"Marissa?"

We whirled around. My heart was in my throat, but I relaxed when I saw it was just Cord. He wasn't alone. He had his arm slung around a slim blonde. She wore skintight white jeans and a bright blue top that flowed over her breasts. They were clearly outlined underneath and it was obvious she wore no bra.

Marissa drew upright. A grim look came over and her eyes hardened. "Are you kidding me?"

"What?" He glanced at the girl who hung on him. "This is Ariella. Have you met her before?"

Marissa's neck vein stood out. For a second, I thought she would launch herself at him. She wouldn't go after the girl, she'd go after him, and I already knew I'd back her up.

"Cord told me he was so nice to go to your little school dance with you. That's so sweet of him." The girl tipped her head back and flipped the hair over her shoulder.

Marissa bared her teeth.

"I just gave him a reward for being so sweet to you." Then Ariella laughed.

The sound traveled down my spine. It was sugary sweet and so fake I had a hard time holding back some laughter. It was so clear that I wondered why Marissa hadn't unleashed her claws and verbally stripped the girl down. She could do it. I had witnessed many times where I had been uncomfortable by how far she would take the verbal beating.

And then she drew back and turned away.

"What?" My mouth fell open as I watched her walk away. Her head was down and she hugged herself as she hurried to her car.

It wasn't long before she drove away.

And then my claws came out. I turned around with heated eyes and glared at Cord. "Are you kidding me?"

The bimbo giggled with delight, but Cord's smirk dropped an inch. "What?" He glared back at me. "Your friend is hot. What do you expect from me? I wanted to bang her, and I did. I never pretended otherwise with her. She knew exactly what I was about when I got a ride down here."

"Why did you agree to go to the dance with her? If that was what you were after, why play it up as some romantic gesture?"

"I was coming anyway. The dance happened to be the same weekend Hunt was coming, so I told her sure. She knew this wasn't anything more than a hook up." He rolled his eyes and then patted the bimbo's rear. "Come on, Ariella." As they walked past, he saluted me. "See you later, Princess."

When they got into a car and drove off, I felt the cold in the air for the first time. I shivered and hurried to the door. Then I really thought about what I was doing there. I didn't know if Jesse was actually in that house, which belonged to a complete stranger.

I wanted to throw my hands in the air in frustration, I had no idea what I was doing. Yet, I still marched up to the front door and pounded my thumb against the doorbell.

It wasn't long before it was thrown open. Some guy in only jeans stood there with a dazed smirk on his face. His hair fell over his eyes and he yelled over his shoulder, "It's a girl!"

A smatter of laughter sounded from inside. Someone yelled back, "Is she hot?"

He looked me up and down. "Yep!"

"Then bring her in!"

More faces peered around the corner, and one of them scrunched up in shock. "Holy hell! That's Ethan Connor's sister."

The guy straightened abruptly. His cocky demeanor vanished. "Oh, hi. I'm Nick. I didn't know who you were." Then he gestured inside. "You can come in, if you want."

I stepped inside. He flattened himself against the wall so there were a few feet between us and closed the door behind me. "Uh, so do you want something to drink?"

"She ain't twenty-one, Jr."

"Oh, yeah." He grinned at me, flustered at the same time. "I think we got soda. Jer!"

"What?"

"We got anything that ain't alcoholic?"

"You want to mix something?" The voice sounded from down a hallway, but it was growing closer. "Otherwise, why would you want something that ain't alcoholic?"

I turned.

Jeremy Benson stood in front of me. His jeans were ripped and unbuttoned. As I glanced around the living room and kitchen, there were a bunch of guys who weren't wearing shirts. Most of them were lean and tanned. A few were built like body builders, but all of them had a beer in hand. The handful of girls

I counted dressed similar to the bimbo from outside. Revealing shirts and revealing pants, if they wore pants at all.

"Hey." Nick pointed at me. "This is Ethan Connor's sister."

"So?" Jeremy skimmed me over with an indifferent look. "I'm not surprised Connor's sister grew up to be hot. You sure you don't want something good to drink? We've got beer, darling, but I've got some good old-fashioned whiskey, too. That's what Barbie drinks."

"Barbie?"

He pointed into the kitchen, and a girl with smoky eyes and dirty blonde hair lifted a hand. "Hi, there." Her voice was hoarse, and she grimaced. "I'm a little hungover. Any friend or relative of Connors is welcome around here."

"Why?"

She frowned but looked over my shoulder.

Jeremy belched out a laugh. He scratched idly at his chest. "What do you mean *why*?"

"I don't remember any of you being friends with Ethan."

Then a wide smile spread over his face and he burst out laughing. Nick laughed with him, along with Barbie and a few others. He shook his head and coughed to clear his throat as he continued to laugh. "Man, I haven't had a good one like that in a while."

"I'm serious."

The smile was wiped away. "Are you kidding me? We were some of the best friends your brother had."

"Jesse was his best friend."

The smirk that appeared over his face made my stomach drop. Dread started to build in me.

"I've got a feeling, darling, that there's a lot you don't know about your big brother."

Barbie draped herself against the doorframe and smirked as well. "I think there's a lot you don't know about the night your big brother died."

Then someone hurried down the stairs. I turned around and froze. Jesse was at the bottom of the stairs behind me, and his eyes were wide as he saw me. The blood drained from his face.

My heart sank into my stomach.

His hand gripped the banister tighter. His knuckles whitened, but then he clipped out, "What the hell are you doing here?"

9

"**H**unt!" Jeremy's voice boomed out. Everyone's attention was now solely on us. He threw his arms wide. One came around my shoulders, and he pulled me tight against his side. "It's Ethan's little sis. You been hiding her from us? What kind of a buddy are you?"

Jesse's eyes narrowed as he straightened to his fullest height. "Get your hands off her."

A shiver went down my spine.

The air in the room, which had been entertaining, grew tense. Jesse's voice was low, deadly low, and the threat of violence filled the room. His hands were clenched in fists, and his eyes sparked with the promise that he would follow through with his threat.

"Well, now." Jeremy's voice grew serious. His arm fell away and he moved to the side. "No need for that. I had no idea she was your girl."

Jesse took two steps and latched on to my arm. He dragged me out the door.

Jeremy hollered from inside, "You don't need to leave, Hunt. We're all friends here."

He gritted his teeth but refrained from responding.

"What are you doing?" I panted as I tried to keep up with him.

His hold on my arm was going to leave a bruise, but I bit my tongue. Jesse looked murderous as he took me to his Ferrari. He opened the door and stepped back. When I didn't get in right away, he snapped, "In! Now."

Anger boiled up inside me, but I got in.

When he got into his own side and took off, I glanced back at my car. This was not the time to remind him that we'd have to come back. I only hoped that Jeremy didn't know it was my car. I hoped they wouldn't do anything to it.

As he sped through town, he took a few corners that had his back end sliding across the road. He didn't slow down. He went faster. The murderous rage in his eyes never diminished either. As he pulled up to the gate in front of his house, he punched a button to open it. Instead of driving up the hill toward the house, he drove underneath it. It was an underground parking garage, and it was filled from one corner to the other with sparkling vehicles.

Jesse pulled up to the front slot and got out. When I shut my door, the sound echoed throughout the space. It only added to my amazement at how big Jesse's home was. Then he went to a door and an elevator opened for him.

I groaned and followed him inside it. My family's house was a typical suburban home, but it was an anthill compared to his. He was still rolling with whatever anger he had over my showing up at Jeremy's house, so I continued to keep my mouth shut.

The elevator opened to a small hallway, and Jesse led us around the corner. We came from a back entryway into the dining room and kitchen area. All the lights were off, but he flipped them all on before he went to one of the large refrigerators.

As he yanked open a door, I slid onto a stool behind one of the counters. "You're going to eat right now?"

He straightened abruptly, closed the door, and glared at me.

I gulped.

"What the hell were you doing there?"

I shrugged. "I heard you were with Benson and Mazel. I came over here because I didn't want you around them. I got the address from somewhere and went over there."

"You got the address?" The muscle in his jaw bulged out. "Where'd you get the address from?"

My eyes slid to the side, and I saw Mary in the hallway. She was pale and she clutched her hands together in front of her. I saw the fear in her eyes as she slowly shook her head.

"Marissa."

He let loose a string of curses and roughly opened the refrigerator again. This time bread, tomatoes, cheese, peppers, and more were thrown on the counter behind him. He slammed the door shut and pulled out a large cutting knife from the block.

I sat up straighter and my eyes widened. "What are you doing with that?"

"I'm making a fucking sandwich. Are you okay with that?" He held the knife in the air, waiting for my approval.

I jerked my head in a nod and watched as he cut the food for his sandwich with a quickness and precision that I'd only witnessed from him on the basketball court. The sight of it made me uneasy, but I held firm. I couldn't let him know that I was uncomfortable. He'd only started to open up. I couldn't risk another closed wall to me. So I sat there and held my breath as he sliced and diced through cheese, peppers, tomatoes, onions, and meat for his sandwich. After he applied some mayonnaise and mustard, I caught my breath again.

That was Ethan's favorite.

I wasn't surprised when Jesse shoved the sandwich in front of me. "Eat!"

I couldn't breathe, but my finger inched the plate away. Then I looked down. "That was Ethan's favorite."

He sucked in his breath and froze.

I'd never seen that look on his face. My hand started to reach for him, but he jerked forward. His arm swept the plate aside and he caught it with his hand before he hurled it at the sink behind him. The entire action was violent, and I fell backward from my stool in shock.

His shoulders heaved up and down. His breathing grew haggard.

I felt the tears on my cheek. I tasted them in my mouth, but I didn't make a sound. Not one sound.

My heart pounded in my chest. It wanted to come out. Each time, it thumped harder and rougher. I pressed my hands to it, trying to calm it, but then Jesse turned back around.

His eyes were dead again.

My chest deflated.

He was back.

The walls were back.

He had no emotion and his voice was soft. "Do you need a ride home?"

I jerked my head from side to side.

He frowned. "You drove to Benson's, didn't you?"

It was jerked in a nod this time.

Then he sighed. His shoulders dropped dramatically. "I should give you a ride back to your car."

As he started to walk back toward the hallway we came from, my mouth fell open. What had just happened? He was there, he was with me and he was present, but now he was gone. In a blink of an eye, he was back to the robotic blank mask he wore to the rest of the world.

As he grabbed his keys, I lunged for them and snatched them from his hand.

He blinked in surprise. "Alex?"

Then I turned and hurled them down the farthest hallway. It was my time to show my anger, and I seethed at him with my hands in fists. My shoulders heaved up and down and my heart threatened to pound itself from my chest again.

"Alex?" He was so quiet, so soft.

"Don't you dare," I snapped at him. I yanked my hands through my hair and pulled at the ends. Pain blasted through me, but I welcomed it. Hell, I relished it. It was a relief. "You make me a sandwich—Ethan's sandwich, and then you push me away again. You don't get to do that anymore. I cared about him, too!"

His face shuttered closed again.

I knew he was going to turn around. As he did, I caught his shoulder and threw him back. Then I pushed him against a wall and yelled in his face, "I loved him, too! He was my brother—"

"He was *my* brother!" His hands found my shoulders, but he held on. "He was there through everything, through my mom, through my dad's affairs. Everything. He was there."

"Say his name."

"What?" He froze.

"Say his name."

His hands dropped as if they'd been burned. He flattened himself against the wall.

"Say his name."

He shook his head.

"Jesse."

Then he brushed past me. I tried to block him, but he kept going and his body hit mine, knocking me backward. I cried out from the pain and fell against the wall, but I couldn't look away. My hand went to my shoulder where it stung, but every cell in my body went on alert. I couldn't look away from the haunted expression in his eyes. He didn't know that he had hurt me. I watched as he seemed locked in some memory. His lips moved, but nothing came out.

I reached out and touched his arm. I pleaded in a tender voice, "Tell me. Please."

He started to shake his head, but his voice wrung out, "I feel him, you know. All the time."

I blinked back rapid tears. "Me, too."

"I feel him at school. I can't get away from him. The only time is when I'm with you." Then he looked up. There was an extra layer of wetness over his eyes. The tears were there, brimming to be shed. "But that makes no sense. I should feel him when I'm with you. You're the only other person to—"

My phone peeled out a shrill ring at that moment. I threw my hands up and let loose a few curses. It was the worst timing, but all the fight left me when I saw who was on the other end. I went numb as I answered it. "Dad?"

"Your, uh . . ." He cleared his throat. His voice sounded rough. "Your mother is in the hospital. She swallowed a bunch of pills."

"What?" I gasped. All thought ceased. Flashbacks from Ethan's accident flooded me, and I struggled to hear what else he was saying.

"Keeping her for observation . . . a seventy-two hour hold . . . coffee . . ."

And then he hung up.

I stared at the phone in my hand. Suddenly, I couldn't remember answering it in the first place, and I frowned at it. What was I doing with my phone? As I looked around, I saw Jesse. His hands were shoved deep in his pockets, and he was watching me with a fierce frown.

Then I remembered.

"What'd your dad want?"

"Ethan was in a car accident." The words spilled from my lips.

Wait—my lips pulled down at the corners. That wasn't right.

I'd been at a party with Marissa and Angie. It was my turn for the drinking game, but the phone pulled me away. It was my dad, and I thought about ignoring him. I was having fun, but then Angie nudged me with her shoulder, silently telling me to answer. He spoke, but his words were fuzzy—too hard to remember.

"Alex." Jesse touched my arm. His voice punching me back to the present day. "What'd your dad say just now?"

I frowned again. Why was this so difficult? "My mother."

"What about her?" He took both of my arms in his hands and bent low so his eyes were level with mine.

I felt him trying to pull me back, but I wasn't sure where from. "She tried to kill herself."

He sucked in his breath and stayed there for a moment. I thought he was going to pull me into his arms, but he didn't. His hands fell away. I was cold without him, but then he stepped farther back.

"I'll take you to the hospital."

I searched his eyes. They were guarded, but it didn't matter anymore. I was surprised as I realized that. I didn't even want to go to the hospital. I'd see her in seventy-two hours. I wouldn't feel her emptiness for three days, and a part of me was relieved. It was a part that I would never share with anyone.

Jesse touched my arm again. "I'll take you."

"Will you stay with me?" I wouldn't go if he wouldn't be there with me.

He nodded. His voice gentled. "I'll stay as long as you need me."

My heart swelled inside, but I reminded myself that he would leave again. Jesse always left. But his hands were gentle as he ushered me out to his car. When we got to the hospital, he went to the front desk and asked the questions I couldn't bear to even form in my mind, and then he led me to the elevator.

I drew in a shuddering breath.

He punched the button for the same floor we'd been on during Ethan's surgery. I couldn't remember if my dad told me she had to have surgery or why.

Then the elevator sounded our arrival and we were walking

down the same hallway as before. It hadn't changed. The walls were white and stark. A few paintings were hung, but they were out of place. And they were in memory of others who had died already.

I shivered. I wondered if I donated one, would it be in Ethan's memory?

"Jesse?"

My father pushed out of his chair. His normally tan face was pale. His features that always seemed charming and charismatic were twisted into a grieving mask, but his eyes lit up when he saw Jesse beside me. Then he had his arms around him and I heard his voice muffled against Jesse's shoulder, "Thank God you've come. It's real good to see you."

Jesse's eyes flashed in confusion at me, but he hugged my father back. When my dad didn't let go, Jesse gave in and hugged him back. After another second, my dad released Jesse, but only to hold him by the shoulders. He shook him a bit. "It's real good to see you. I mean that. How have you been?"

I saw that Jesse swallowed tears back. His head nodded and then hung.

My dad hugged him again. This time was longer, as if Jesse had been the one who died and came back to life.

After the second hug, Jesse asked hoarsely, "How's Shelby?"

"Oh." My dad's arms fell away. He shook his head and the same hoarseness came to his voice. "She ain't doing good. She's in surgery right now. They had to pump her stomach, and I guess she swallowed a razorblade, too. I don't know anything else yet."

Jesse looked at me in question.

I flinched as I knew what he was thinking. Why hadn't I told him before? He knew my mother would've shown signs of depression before, but how was I supposed to answer that? We were all sad. We'd been sad for so long. It hadn't only been her.

I turned away and found an empty seat. Then I huddled in my own corner. My father never once looked at me. When he saw

Jesse, his eyes were only for him. That was when I knew that I'd been right. He loved Jesse more than he loved me. Jesse was his last real connection to Ethan.

As we waited to hear how the surgery went, my dad talked only to Jesse. They hugged a few more times, and then Jesse took the seat beside me. He relayed everything my father told him.

After the sixth hour of being there, the doctor came out. My father motioned for Jesse to approach the doctor with him. I couldn't even find it in me to be bothered by that. And again, Jesse came back to me. The surgery had gone well. My mother would be held for observation and placed under suicide watch and would be monitored closely.

It'd be weeks before she would return home.

I knew the instant my father had told Jesse that. The relief in his eyes was unmistakable, and as Jesse explained it all to me, I shared the same sentiment.

I could be at home and not feel her emptiness.

Finally.

I would only feel my own since my father was rarely home. He spent most of his time at the office, and he'd likely spend the rest of the time at the hospital with my mother.

A different sense of numbness settled in me as Jesse bundled me back in my coat. He hugged my father another time, and after my dad thumped him on the back, with his voice full of emotion as he thanked him for coming in a voice full of emotion, Jesse led me back to that same elevator we had taken up.

We were leaving again, but my mother was still alive. Ethan had died. My mother would live.

I didn't feel any of it.

When we got to my home, Jesse sat me at the kitchen table. A cup of water was placed in front of me, along with some toast. I nibbled on a piece because he had that determined look in his eyes. When I was done and shoved the plate aside, Jesse sighed, but he took it to the sink and led me by my hand to my room.

No words were shared as I got ready for bed.

Jesse helped me get ready for bed.

He found my pajamas and helped me put them on. When I felt the warm material against my skin, my eyes closed. I readied myself. He would leave soon. I looked at the bed. I already knew I wouldn't sleep at all. When I glanced back to him, he was pulling his sweater off. I moved to the dresser and pulled open the bottom drawer, retrieving the shirt he had left here the first time we had ever been together. He slipped it over his head and undid his pants. When he saw that I was staring, he gave me a crooked grin.

"You thought I was going to leave?"

I nodded.

I couldn't speak.

I hadn't been able to since the phone call.

Then he cupped both sides of my face and stepped close, making sure I was looking in his eyes before he spoke. "I will stay as long as you need me."

I choked out, my voice raw and painful, "I thought you'd leave. There's a lot of feeling tonight."

His thumb brushed over my cheek. It was a tender gesture. "Not for you. You turned it off tonight, didn't you?"

Then the tears came. I couldn't stop them. I didn't know what unleashed them, but they fell free like a waterfall.

Jesse cursed under his breath but held me against him. He rocked me back and forth for a while, eventually picking me up and laying me in bed. I fell asleep tucked in his arms with more tears on my cheeks. Sometime during the night, I woke. The tears had dried on my face, but I brushed them away and found that I was alone in the bed.

An eerie feeling came over me, and I left for the hallway. The bathroom was empty, and there were no lights on in the house. I didn't search downstairs, though. I already knew where he was. I stopped outside of Ethan's bedroom. The door was open and I saw Jesse on the edge of his bed. His elbows were braced on his knees and his head was bowed, resting in the palms of his hands. His shoulders shook. There was no sound, but I knew he was sobbing.

My heart broke then. I thought it'd been broken already, but it splintered apart again. Then I stopped thinking and went inside. As Jesse had comforted me before, I did the same. I lifted his head and slid between his arms. His whole body stiffened for the briefest of moments before he lifted me on his lap. My legs parted, and I straddled him, needing to hold him close. Desire burst forth in me when I saw the heat in his eyes. He didn't want comfort. He wanted to forget.

His hands cupped my legs. He pulled me tight and ground into me. My chest was pressed against his, and my lips parted for him.

We both forgot together.

10

We woke around nine the next morning. I was the first to wake. I couldn't stay in bed any longer; too many memories haunted me because of the night before, so I got out of bed. When I came back from showering, I saw that Jesse was dressed. As we bypassed the kitchen, I thought about making coffee, but Jesse touched my arm.

"I'll make some at my place for you."

And that was that. We went to get my car, which had been left alone. Thank goodness. And I followed Jesse back to his house. When he drove into the basement parking area, I waited and drove up the driveway to his front door. I waited outside for him to come, but the door opened. His housekeeper, Mary, motioned for me to come in. Her plump cheeks were flushed. Her dimples appeared and I grinned back at her. She squeezed my arm once, but never said anything.

"Jesse?"

She pointed toward the kitchen, so I led the way.

Jesse grinned when he saw both of us. He waved toward the table. "Sit. I'll make breakfast."

Mary and I sat at the table as he made breakfast for us both. We had toast, eggs, and bacon. He made the coffee he had promised. Mary got up from the table. She came back with creamer and sugar. I was about to say thank you, but she dumped a bunch in her own coffee and then plopped them back on the table.

Jesse took the seat beside mine with his own plate of food, and the three of us ate in silence. When Mary finished first, she got up, collected all the dirty dishes, and took them back into the kitchen. Jesse tapped my hand, and I followed him to his room. It was then I realized that was a normal routine for the two of them.

It was something I hadn't expected from him, but then again, my family had been like his most of his life. It made sense that he had sought out that type of comfortable relationship with Mary. She'd been with his family as long as I could remember.

When we got to his room, I curled up on his bed and watched as he started to pack his clothes. And then a different thought came to me. "Why didn't you say anything when Marissa was calling you all the time?"

The shirt he had grabbed was balled into his fist when he turned to look at me. A flare of guilt flashed in his eyes before it was gone. "Why would I?"

I felt punched in the gut, but then I sighed. Had I really expected anything less? "No, I mean, was she bothering you?"

He shrugged but turned away and disappeared into his closet again. It was a while before he came back out. This time he had a pile of clothes in his arms and he dropped them all on the bed. As he started to fold them, he bit out, "You're not my girlfriend, Alex. That's not what this is."

"I know it's not." I said that slowly and casually, but I couldn't lie to myself. The rejection stung. It stung a whole bunch after the night we'd just shared together.

When he didn't say anything further, I sat up and hugged my knees to my chest. "I saw you at that movie premiere, you know."

"No, I don't." He grinned, but it fell a second later. "Whatever. I was there for my dad. He'd been harassing me to go to one of his movies, so I figured I'd do it to shut him up."

"Did it work?"

"No." He sighed and reached for some more shirts to fold. "He's pushing my name around with his business. I think he's hoping I'll go pro early and get some promotion deals or something."

"Would you want to do that?" I asked, though I knew he wouldn't.

Disbelief flared in his eyes. "Are you kidding me?"

I grinned. "Yeah, actually."

He shook his head. "I hate that business." He glanced at his watch. "Ass Face is coming home tonight. I'd better get a move on it if I want to avoid him."

"Why'd you come home this weekend?"

He shrugged and glanced around the room. "I think I have almost everything," he said as an answer as he headed into the bathroom. He had a little bag in hand when he returned. He placed it in the big one and yawned, scanning the room for a second time.

I swallowed tightly and took a breath. "Are you coming home for Thanksgiving break?"

He shook his head. One of his hands idly scratched at his chest. I knew he was still thinking about if he had everything before he left. He murmured, "Practices already started. We got games during that time. Am I forgetting anything?"

I had so many answers for that question, but I held them all back.

Then he sighed again and found me with his gaze. His eyes narrowed. "Are you going to date that second stringer?"

"Eric Nathan?"

"Yeah." He frowned. "You going to be manned-up the next time I come to town?"

I shrugged. At this point, I had no idea.

He continued to frown as he stared at me.

"What?"

His eyes narrowed farther. "Are there any other guys I don't know about?"

I shrugged again. "I don't think anyone else likes me, if that's what you're asking."

He grunted. Then he sat beside me on the bed. "They like you, Alex. I know a whole bunch of them like you. They *more* than like you."

"Did you meet anyone at that movie premiere? I'm sure there are lots of gorgeous actresses and models at events like that."

He gave me a rueful grin.

"What?"

Then he chuckled. He swung an arm around my shoulders and pulled me close. His breath fanned my cheek as he continued to chuckle into my ear. "Are you jealous, Alex?"

I nudged him with my elbow, but I knew my cheeks were aflame.

He hugged me tight again before he pressed a kiss to my fore-head. "Are you trying to see if I'm seeing anyone?"

I gestured to the bed. "We're not exactly just friends, Jesse."

"Yeah, I know." His arm dropped from my shoulder and his tone sobered. "Man, I know." He raked a hand over his head, sighed, and then turned on the bed so he was facing me squarely. One of his legs trapped me closer, and he cupped both sides of my face. "I won't lie to you. I don't know what we are, but we're not exclusive. I can't handle that. I've slept with two girls since I got to school."

My heart stopped.

"But they were just hook-ups and didn't mean anything. It was empty sex—that was it. I don't want a girlfriend. I can't do that, and if that's where you want this to go, we need to stop right now. I can't lose you in my life, and I won't risk it because of that. Sex is one thing, but sex before our friendship is another thing."

I couldn't breathe.

His thumb started to rub back and forth. He choked out, "So what do you think?"

About what?

There wasn't a choice given to me.

I couldn't look away from him. I swore I wasn't imagining the flare of pain that flashed in his eyes before it was gone. It was so quick, so fleeting that I could've mistaken it for something else. I continued to hold my breath. What do I do? The choice was in my hands. Keep it as it is or drop it.

I whispered, "I can't stop this."

He let out a soft sigh.

"I should." Pain flared in my chest before tightening around my heart. "I think Eric would like to be my boyfriend. He won't hurt me like you do. You always leave me, Jesse. You blow into my life and then you leave every time. We *should* stop this. We should stop it right now."

A haunted look came to him.

My heart skipped a beat. He felt something for me. I knew it. I almost relished in it, but then I deflated once again. It didn't matter. He said it himself. He didn't want a girlfriend, and no matter what he felt for me, I knew he wouldn't allow it. He wouldn't let it grow into something more. I also wasn't able to walk away. One day I would. I knew I'd be strong enough to leave the shelter he gave me, but not that day, not at that minute.

I still needed him.

"What do you want, Alex?" It looked like that question cost him. He seemed in pain.

I shook my head. A tear slipped down my cheek. "I can't."

His forehead dropped to mine.

My hands lifted to his shoulders, and I hung on. I was helpless at that moment as I confessed, "I can't stop this, not yet."

Then his lips caught mine. I surged against him as I wrapped my arms around him, pulling him close. Like all the other times, time ceased for us. It was only the two of us and the frenzied need we felt for the other.

Later that night as I got ready for bed and Jesse had gone, my phone beeped a few times. One was from Angie. She wanted to know how I was and if I had heard from Marissa. The next was from Eric. He hoped I had a good weekend and the third was from Jesse. He hoped my mother was okay, and he would come back for Christmas break. My phone beeped a fourth time. It was from him again.

Jesse: Don't have a boyfriend when I come back.

I thumbed a quick response to Angie, telling her that I hadn't heard from Marissa. I didn't tell her about what happened with Cord. That was for Marissa to tell her. My next response was to Eric. I replied that the weekend went fast, and I hoped he had a good one as well. Then my last response was to Jesse.

Me: Okay.

That it was, nothing more. I didn't feel he needed more than that.

Angie and Eric both responded a few times before I crawled into bed. It wasn't until I turned the light off and settled underneath my comforter that I got his reply.

Jesse: Good.

In some ways my world was crumbling around me, but that night I went to bed with a smile. I couldn't stop my smile, and I had a strong sense that Ethan was smiling as well, wherever he was.

❧

MY MOTHER HAD BEEN in the hospital for two weeks. I visited her once, but her eyes had been vacant the whole time. One of the nurses advised against any more returns from me. Apparently, her blood pressure and heart rate had skyrocketed when I was there. It was calm when my father was there, which was so often that they had actually brought a cot for him to sleep on. When I'd gone into her bathroom, my dad's toiletry bag was on a shelf inside.

After I left, I sat in my car with my phone in my hand. I had considered calling Jesse, but what could he say? Besides the one text message, he hadn't commented about my mother that weekend or since then. And I couldn't call anyone else. I hadn't told anyone about my mother. I wasn't about to start. My family had enough grief, and I couldn't stomach any more sympathy.

But it didn't last long.

"Hey!" Angie slapped a hand on my locker. She shut it for me as I stepped back with my bag over my shoulder.

"Thanks." I watched it close and turned for the parking lot.

"Hey!" she said again before she fell in step beside me. Then she lowered her voice. "You didn't tell me about your mother. She's in the hospital? Alex! How could you not tell me that?"

I shrugged and veered around two freshmen girls. When they started giggling, I looked up and saw the reason for it. Eric was at the end of the hallway with some of his teammates. All of them wore their letterman jackets and lounged against the wall as if they owned the place. Then I sighed. In some ways, they might've. The freshmen girls would've attested to that fact.

When Eric caught sight of me, his face lit up and he lifted a hand.

I nudged Angie with my elbow. "Can we not talk about my mom? I didn't say anything because it's . . ." I hesitated. What could I say? I couldn't tell her that it'd been a relief for me that she was gone from the house. That didn't sound appropriate. "It's just a lot, okay? It's too much sometimes."

Her face sagged. She caught my shoulders with her hands and stopped me. "I'm so sorry, Alex. I really am. If you need anything at all, call me! Seriously. My mom is making lasagna tonight. Come over for dinner?"

"Hey, guys." Eric approached, his voice was cheerful.

Angie ignored him. "What do you say?"

"Say to what?" He moved closer and lowered his head.

I sighed and then relented. "Sure."

"Great!" Her smile was radiant before she bounded off. She hollered back from the door, "Come at eight. We'll go bowling with Justin and the gang after."

I gave her a thumbs-up in response, but it was weak. My smile wavered.

Then she was out the door, and I gave Eric the same weak smile as I'd given her. "Hey."

"You're going bowling tonight?"

He sounded cheerful, too cheerful. After Jesse's last text message, I'd been able to evade Eric most of the time. There'd been almost no alone time with us, and I knew he wouldn't pursue a date with me through a note, so I figured I was in the clear. Until now. We were alone.

"Hey, girlfriend!" Marissa smacked my butt and bounced to a halt beside us. Her eyes went from eager to sultry as she scanned Eric up and down. "What are you doing tonight, Eric?'

His eyes widened a fraction, and his hands gripped his book bag tighter. "I'm . . ." His eyes darted to me with a question in them.

"He's going bowling with me and Angie and the gang."

His grin grew and two dimples appeared.

Marissa melted at the sight. "Great! Pick me up at nine, Eric?"

"Uh." He looked stricken as his eyes skirted from me to her. "I'm, uh, sure."

"See you later!" She winked at him before she was grabbed by some of her cheerleading friends. They led her away, but their giggling grew in volume after she whispered something to them.

When all of them stopped and looked at us, Eric staggered back a step.

Then they disappeared around a corner.

"What just happened there?" He scratched the top of his head.

I chuckled and started forward. "You have a date with Marissa if I'm not mistaken."

He groaned but fell in step with me. "How did that happen?"

"She set her sights on you and down you folded. Good luck with that one."

"She's your best friend, right?" He watched me from the corner of his eye as we turned toward my car.

"Yep. Hurt her and die."

He groaned again. "I meant to ask you out, and instead, I'm being threatened by you. I don't think I'll ever understand girls." Then he grew serious and stopped us. "I can't ask you out now, can I?"

I shook my head.

Frustration flared across his features as he pinched the top of his nose. "I have horrible luck with girls. I'm cursed. That's it. I have to be cursed."

I patted him on the arm. "Well, if you're not serious about her, Marissa has the attention span of a bee for guys. She'll be buzzing around someone else in a week. I'm sure of it."

"A bee, huh?" He relaxed a little.

"Don't let her know I told you that."

He shot me a grin. "I won't. And I'll see you tonight." He gave me a playful bow before he turned toward his truck. As he went, I watched how he continued to scratch the top of his head and I couldn't hold back a grin. For once, I was glad for Marissa's man eating ways.

She did me a favor.

Eric wouldn't ask me out for a while again and I could hold on to the promise I'd given Jesse, even though I knew I didn't need to. I wasn't going to be his girlfriend. That wasn't what I was holding out for. I was waiting for one last time to be in his arms, one last time to be connected with him again. And it wasn't about sex. It was more than that for me.

I shivered in anticipation. Christmas break couldn't come quick enough.

11

My mom came home a month later, in time for the Thanksgiving holiday. However, when the bell rang on that last day and I knew I had four days of freedom, I wasn't thrilled. Everyone else was giddy. They loved the days away from school. They loved being able to sleep in and they loved all the food and family time.

Not me.

School was my retreat from the house. And sleep still escaped me most nights. As for the food and family time, I overheard my dad on the phone in his office one night. He was booking two plane tickets for the Caribbean for him and my mother. The two of them could heal together and escape another Thanksgiving without Ethan.

The one thing I looked forward to was Jesse's basketball game. It was going to be televised on Friday. I had the whole day planned. I was going to sleep as long as I could, I was going to get coffee, maybe some popcorn, and then I was going to take my blankets to the couch. I would wait for his game for the entire day if I had to.

As I headed to my car on Wednesday, Marissa bounded up to me and hooked her elbow through mine. She panted and gave me a silly smile while she smoothed some of her sleek black hair down from the wind. "Whatcha doing, buddy?"

I hid my grin. She'd been cautious with me since she had started dating Eric. The two of them had been enjoyable to watch at bowling that night. She'd been flirty and seductive while he had stumbled over his feet more than a few times. It was a month into their relationship. She seemed happier than I'd ever seen her.

"Not much."

Her smile kicked up a notch. "Okay, can I ask you a favor?"

When wouldn't she? I shrugged. "Sure. Why not?"

"Are you doing anything tomorrow?"

"Besides eating turkey with my parents?" I had to fake it. No one knew how pathetic my family life had become. "Not much. Why?"

"Can I tell my parents that I'm going to have Thanksgiving at your house? I know it's a lot to ask, but I got two tickets on discount for Vegas. It's not Hawaii or anything, but it's something special. I really, really like Eric. He's going to tell his parents that he'll have his meal at your place, too. It'll be like a friends thing with your folks. Can we do that? Can we use your place as an excuse? You'll cover for us if they call?"

Sometimes I had to shake my head at my own stupidity, but I nodded. "Sure."

"Oh, thank you, thank you, thank you, Alex!" She bounced up and gave me a tight hug. "This means the world. You don't even know it."

The glow on her face was unmistakable. I couldn't help myself from asking, "Do you have something special planned for the trip?"

Her mouth clamped shut and her cheeks reddened. But her

eyes sparkled. They seemed so alive, which was something I hadn't seen in her since Cord had shattered her.

"Well?"

She giggled and leaned close. "We're going to do it."

"It?" I frowned. I thought Marissa would've had sex with him by now. I loved my friend and all, but she wasn't known for taking a month to get underneath the covers. "You haven't had sex yet?"

She bit her lip as she shook her head. "I know. I know. But after Cord, I wanted to take my time and make sure this was the right guy."

"And is he?"

Her head bobbed up and down. "I think so. I really do. I can't believe I'm saying this, but I think I might be in love with him. Can you believe it?"

My grin faltered. She had been in love with Cord, too. But then a little hope lit inside me. Did it change so quickly? Could I feel the same for someone else after my last time with Jesse? Maybe things weren't so depressing for me. I could fall in love again . . . but as I considered that, I knew I wasn't wired the same as her. It wouldn't be that easy for me and I really didn't know if I could fall in love with someone else, especially that quick. It'd only been a month for her.

"Okay. I'll see you later!" She gave me another cheerful wave before she skipped away. I was sure she was going to find Eric and share the good news of their lie.

"Ugh," Angie groaned as she sidled up next to me and stared off in the direction Marissa just disappeared. "Why am I friends with her? Seriously. I have no idea. She has no idea of what loyalty means. I don't think she's capable of empathy. Why are we both friends with her?"

I shrugged. "Because she's got our backs at times and because we both love her, faults and all."

She tipped her head back and let loose a loud sigh. "I have no idea how you can stand her. She craps on you more than anyone else, I swear. And she'd crap on me if I weren't with Justin. Remember how she used to flirt with him? I'm going to drop kick her head one of these days and finally score that goal the football team should've got our last game." She patted her chest. "Me. I'll do that. And I'll enjoy it."

"Stop." I nudged her with my elbow. "If I really liked Eric, she—"

"She would've still gone after him."

That stopped me, but I wasn't going to let it depress me. There was already a list she had no idea about, Marissa wasn't anywhere on it.

I hooked my elbow through hers and dragged her to my car. "Can we talk about something else? Marissa's love life can be tiring at times."

"I know. I'm sorry. You're a better friend than me."

"Not really. I'm just not that mad because she helped me out without realizing it."

"She did?" Angie's eyebrow arched high. Her hand found her hip. "How so?"

I shrugged. Did I really want to get into this? "I was avoiding Eric. I'm not ready for a relationship."

"And she took him off your hands?" She pursed her lips together and shook her head. "It wasn't even like that, Alex. She took your man. If she wanted him, she should've asked for your permission. She did none of that, and she's been hiding from you the past month tells me she's guilty. She's not that good of a friend."

I sighed. This wasn't going to go anywhere productive, so I purposely lightened my tone. "What are your plans for the break?"

Her eyes stayed narrowed and she kept them trained on me. She stared and stared some more. Finally, she rolled them and sighed in disgust. "You are so infuriating sometimes. You should be mad as hell and instead you're over here, Miss Little Forgiveness. How can you sleep at night? With halos over your head? Or are you keeping secrets, too?"

I froze. My heart stopped for a second.

Her hand went in the air, and she groaned again. "And now I'm being the horrible friend. I feel like I have to be perfect to catch up with you. You're so damn holy and selfless. What the hell's wrong with you?"

I stared at her.

She cringed. "Jesus. Don't listen to me. I'm cursing, using His name in vain. I'm the one going to hell. Marissa will get away scot-free, but not me. I'll be going down South while she folds her wings around her and floats to heaven, all innocent and crap when we both know she's not."

I laughed, but I couldn't help but feel some of my own guilt. Mine might not have been the type of secrets to hurt anyone else, but they were still secrets. And one of them was how I was going to spend my Thanksgiving. I shook my head and plastered a fake smile on my face. "What are your plans for the break?"

"Yeah, yeah. I heard you the first time. I'm just so damn irritated with Marissa. She's getting away with being a really crappy friend and the one person she shouldn't be crappy to, is you. But you won't say anything."

Because I had my own lies. But I held my tongue.

Then she cursed under her breath and sighed. "Okay. What'd you ask? Oh, my break. I don't know. Family thing tomorrow. Justin will be around. That's all I have planned. I think we're going to his house tomorrow night for family game night. You?"

I lied through my teeth. "Family dinner, that's it."

"Oh. Well. I'm sure that time together will be good for you guys." Then a different look came to her. It was more serious, deeper, and it sent a kick to my stomach. I readied myself when I heard her ask, "Why haven't you said anything about your mom? I know that I know, but no one else knows. I mean, my word, Alex. You've had a hard time the past year and a half, and now your mom was in the hospital. I think you should say something."

I blinked back a sudden rush of tears. The sympathy loosened them, but I hardened myself. Crying never fixed anything and I didn't want to appear weak. No one would respect me after that, and that was all I had left. I shook my head, forcing my voice to sound normal. "No, I can't. It's all right. My mom's a lot better."

She sighed again, and then wiped her own tear away. "I'm sorry. I am. I just . . ." But she bit her lip and turned away. Her shoulders shook a bit, but I waited with a knot in my stomach until she turned back. Her voice rose on a sob, "I just can't imagine if that'd been my mom. I would've lost it. I know I would've."

And that was the gist of it. As I heard her, the truth startled me. I had lost my mom when I had lost Ethan. I had lost my father as well. I'd lost my whole family. I still had Jesse, in some ways, but nothing was the same. *I* wasn't the same.

When Angie grasped my arm, I jerked back to our conversation. I was shaken as I realized a few tears had slipped past my eyes. They streamed down my cheek, but Angie had her own. She pulled me in for a hug and whispered in my ear, "I love you. You know that, right? I really do. If you need anything, anything at all, please, please, please call me. Please, Alex."

I hugged her back and nodded, but when she didn't let go, my arms tightened around her. And then I found myself hugging her back as much as she did with me. Something loosened in me. I didn't know what it was, but it was something and it was important. When I felt more tears coming, I pulled back and brushed them away. I couldn't lose it. I didn't know if I'd put it all back together again.

Her hand fell to my arm. "I just feel that you're hurting a lot more than you let on and it kills me. You've always been a great friend and have been there for me. You deserve that back, you deserve more than that."

I grasped her hand in mine and squeezed it tight.

Then Angie groaned. "Oh hell. Look at us. We both look like blathering idiots. Where's that passive aggressive bitch Sarah Shastaine at a moment like this? She'd wet herself, I swear."

Some laughter ripped out of me. My eyes went wide, but then I couldn't stop laughing. And Angie joined in. Both of us were giggling so much, we were drawing attention. It wasn't long until Justin found his way over to us. A perplexed look was on his face as he knelt and slung Angie's bag over his shoulder. "You guys aren't high, are you?"

Angie snorted and swatted at his shoulder.

We laughed harder at that.

Then he shook his head and sighed. "Okay. I'll see you at the car, honey."

She nodded. "Oh, my word. That felt good, painful but good."

I nodded, grinning like an idiot.

"Okay." She hugged me once more and took a breath. "I'll see you later. Call me if you're bored and want to get out of the house tomorrow. Otherwise, there's a party Friday. We'll pick you up at six for that."

"What—no—"

But it didn't matter. Angie gave me another wave and headed across the parking lot for Justin's truck. As she rushed him and threw her arms around his shoulders, pain seared inside my chest. They were happy. They were in love. I wanted that, but I'd never get it. Another flare of pain surged through me, but I stopped it. I put it on hold and pushed everything down inside me. Self pity wouldn't get me anywhere, and right now, I needed to survive.

And then I got into my car and headed home to an empty house.

When I got home, I found a note from my dad. He had gone

to pick up my mom from the hospital and they were going straight to the airport from there. And then I got another surprise. They would be gone for over two weeks. Apparently, my mother needed a vacation; it was a long awaited one for the both of them, and they would see me when they returned. A last line of the note told me not to get in trouble.

Trouble?

What trouble would they even care about now?

Then I remembered Angie's hug and her words. *I just feel that you're hurting a lot more than you let on and it kills me.* When the same tears came to the surface, I brushed them away and headed to my room. It wasn't near evening, but I changed into my pajamas and curled underneath my covers. I had texted my friends that my mom was out of the hospital, but I didn't text them anything else. At this point, I didn't know what was worse. Having my mom in the house when I knew she was suffering like the rest of us, or not having anyone here at all. I gulped, being alone in the house when I felt Ethan's presence was so over-whelming sometimes I could only gasp for breath and hold on to where I was at the moment. Sometimes I was in bed. Sometimes I was at the kitchen table, gripping the table in front of me. When I was on the couch, I hugged the cushion. By the time it would leave me, I was so shaken and pale that I was sure I looked like a ghost myself.

I always wanted to call Jesse, but I never did. I did now, though. I gave in, but I hung up almost as soon as the line started to ring. No good would come from hearing his voice. Only pain.

I sighed and stuffed all the pain down again.

I'd been doing it for over a year.

And with that last thought, I took a deep breath and then put a movie in. It was after my fourth one when the doorbell rang, my cell phone buzzed an alert, and my parents' landline rang. I jumped and hoped I hadn't crapped my pants. I threw back the covers and hurried downstairs. The phone kept ringing, so I grabbed that one first.

"Hello?"

"It's me." Angie sounded out of breath.

The doorbell went again.

"Someone's at the door. I'll call you back in a second."

"It's me. I'm freezing my ass off."

"Oh—" I hung up and went to the door. As I swung it open, a burst of cold air blasted me. Angie and Justin were both shivering and dashed inside. I was pushed against the wall, but when I followed them into the living room, I couldn't hold back a smile. Angie dove for the blankets and wrapped one around her shoulders before she hurled herself on the couch. Justin gave me a slight wave as he was stomping his feet up and down and shaking his hands.

"What are you guys doing here?"

Angie rolled to her back on the couch and grinned up at me. She was cocooned like a butterfly. "Marissa called. She found another good deal. Pack your bags. Our plane leaves for Vegas in three hours."

"What? No."

"Come on."

"No."

"Yes."

I opened my mouth, a lame excuse on the tip of my tongue, when Angie rolled her eyes and struggled to sit up. Then she made a show of looking around. I closed my mouth. I already knew where this was going. I beat her to it. "It's date night."

She snorted. "Yeah, right. No one's here."

"I told you. Date night. They're allowed."

Her eyes narrowed. "When are they coming back?"

"Tonight."

"Fine." There was movement under her blanket and I guessed

it was her arms crossing over her chest. "Then we'll stay and wish them Happy Thanksgiving."

My eyes narrowed and I spoke through gritted teeth, "They're coming back tomorrow, but I'm not supposed to tell anybody that."

"Why not?"

"They don't want overnight guests." I cringed at that lie. It wasn't even a believable one.

"And what overnight guests wouldn't they like? Me? Since when do they not like me?"

I glanced around for Justin, but he was gone. Not a surprise. He had a habit of wandering anywhere we would go. "What's the point of this? I don't want to go to Vegas. I can't afford it."

"I told you. It's a good deal."

I sighed, "I still can't. I have no money."

"What about the Coffee Hut?"

"Minimum wage?"

She flinched. "You're right, but that's okay. It's my treat. I owe you for all the years of great friendship."

And then Justin came back in with a note in his hand. He held it up with a weird expression on his face. "Since when does date night consist of two weeks?"

My stomach hurled to the ground.

Angie's mouth dropped open.

I hissed at him, "What are you? A ninja? Stop poking through my house."

He shrugged as Angie threw the blanket off and snatched the note from his hand. Then she cried out, "Are you serious? Your parents left you alone for two weeks? That's insane."

"It's no big deal."

"No big deal? It's a huge deal. That decides it. Shoo. Go pack a bag for the weekend. We're all going to Vegas."

I folded my arms over my chest and dug my heels in. "I'm fine being alone."

She snorted again.

"I am. I have a whole day planned tomorrow."

"What? Eating? Maybe sleeping?"

She wasn't far off, but I puffed my chest out and tried on my best indignant expression. "No, I was going to watch Jesse's game tomorrow. It's being televised."

"Well, guess what?" Her eyes gleamed at me with purpose.

I was suddenly nervous.

"You can actually go to his game. They play in Vegas, and Marissa's already got tickets for us. She said Cord owed her and he's on the team, so what's your next argument with that?"

She'd beaten me. Or the idea of seeing Jesse again had done the trick. I tried to tell myself that I was going to pack a bag because Angie had won this argument. Then I shook my head, and my heart picked up its pace. I couldn't lie to myself. I was going to see Jesse. The idea had my hands sweating already.

"Fine." I said it slowly and oh so reluctantly.

She smirked. "And don't even try to pretend that you're not excited about seeing your guy again. We all know differently."

I froze. What did she know?

Then she admitted, "I'm a little excited to see him play. He's our hometown celebrity. Maybe we should ask for his autograph."

Justin frowned. "I don't like that idea."

Angie laughed before she draped herself over him, fluttered her eyelashes, and pressed a kiss to his cheek. "Oh, come on. I love you, but Jesse Hunt is gorgeous."

A small grin escaped his frown. "I have a little bit of a man crush on him. I'm man enough to admit that."

As I went up to my room, I couldn't hold back my smile. I was excited. I wasn't even going to try to stuff it down. It was the first time in a long time I'd felt that emotion. When I checked my cell phone, I got even more excited. It was a text message from Jesse, but then I read it.

Jesse: U in Vegas? Your folks are here, said they stopped in for a few days before some trip? U here? Call me.

I plopped down on my bed.

Everything went numb. The phone fell from my hand, and I couldn't do anything. I sat there. And I didn't know how long I was there before Angie poked her head around the door. She had a wide smile on her face, but it vanished in a heartbeat. She pushed through the door and sat beside me. "What's wrong?"

I shook my head. I couldn't speak.

Then she bent and lifted the phone from the floor. After she read the text, she studied me for a moment. Her voice was so small when she asked, "You didn't know they were going there?"

I shook my head. I still couldn't speak.

"How long has this been going on?"

Everything in me throbbed. My heart ached. My head hurt. I couldn't get my fingers to work, but I rasped out, "What?"

She lifted my phone. "Your parents. They up and left you. Now they went to see Jesse and you didn't even know. Or did you?"

I shook my head. Why did everything hurt? It always hurt.

She sighed. It was a soft sigh, one that spoke of so much emotion. "I'm sorry, Alex. I really am."

I jerked a shoulder up. What did it matter?

Then she asked the question I'd been dreading. "How long have you and Jesse been texting?"

My eyes closed.

She watched me. I felt her gaze. And I shook my head. This wasn't the time to push that button, and she knew it. "Okay. I'll leave that one alone, but I'm going to ask you later. You know I will."

I nodded as I bit my lip. Even that slight bit of pain was welcomed. It distracted from the other pain inside me. I was help-less against that form.

One of Angie's hands caught the side of my head and she

pulled me against hers in a sideways hug. "I'm sorry, Alex. I really am for what I can't even imagine has happened."

My eyes clasped shut. The tears were there, they wanted to cascade out, but I couldn't let them. It'd be over if I did. I'd been holding everything in so well until then. I couldn't break.

But my hand grasped her arm, and I held on tight. I didn't want to move away, not in this lifetime.

12

My stomach was twisting the entire time on the plane, and it didn't take long for us to get our bags or grab a taxi to the hotel Marissa booked. As we got closer to the Tropicana, my heart was pumping louder and louder. I couldn't believe Angie or Justin hadn't heard it.

When the taxi got to the hotel and we walked into the lobby, Marissa and Eric were waiting for us. She jumped up and down, waving her hand. As she lifted her arm each time, her white dress inched up a centimeter with each wave.

"You're here! You're here." Marissa clapped. "Yay, yay!"

Eric looked green around his mouth. He held a hand to his stomach but tried for a smile. "Hey, guys."

Angie's eyebrows went high. "And she's drunk."

Justin chuckled and clapped a hand on Eric's shoulder. "Got a guy to get you booze. Been drinking since you got here?"

He nodded, and gulped for breath. His cheeks swelled suddenly.

Justin's laugh grew in volume. He swatted him once again. "Yep, sounds like Marissa's influence has done its job. Good job."

Eric jerked forward, clapped a hand over his mouth, paled, and then fled down a hallway.

"Honey!" Marissa followed after him with clumsier movements.

"Hey! What about us?"

"Oh." She put the brakes on and skidded back. A key card was flung at us from her purse before she turned back around. "You're all in room 5214, right next to us. You're checked in and everything. I'll come over in a bit."

"All of us?"

A distracted wave was her response.

Angie sighed in disgust. "I can't believe she did that. We should've gotten a suite with three separate rooms. That would be less awkward then."

"Uh . . ." Justin glanced at me from the corner of his eye. "Um, honey. We'll be fine. It's no problem."

"No problem?" she seethed. "This is all Marissa's fault. She called us at the last minute and demanded we all do this, and then she doesn't think things through. Honey, we're in Vegas and we can't—"

Then she stopped and turned to me wide eyed.

My chest felt like it was trying to burrow in on itself, but I swallowed my pride and shrugged. "It's fine. I can get my own room somewhere."

"Oh, my God. I am so sorry, Alex. I didn't mean—" She balled up her fists and pressed them to her forehead. "None of this is going the right way. I can't believe I said it like that. I'm really sorry, Alex. I really am. I'm mad at Marissa, not you, never you."

But, I *was* the problem. And she knew that I knew that. A deep guilt started to settle in when Justin threw his arms around us both and pulled us tight. He squeezed us together and said in a cheerful tone, "No worries, Alex. Ang and I can have daytime sex if you're not around."

"Justin!"

He grinned at me as he was swatted in the back of his head. "I prefer sex during the day anyway, so you're kind of helping me out here."

"Shut up, Justin."

He just hugged us tighter and turned both of us toward the hallway. "Come on, ladies. Let's go find our room."

Angie glared at him. "I'm going to make you pay for this, you know."

"Yeah, but that's another reason why having Alex around is a good idea for me. You can't fillet my ass if there is a witness."

She opened her mouth, ready for another seething retort, but then she jerked in the air and gasped. She whirled around, red in the face and eyes as a hand reached around to her butt. Her mouth opened and closed like a goldfish's for a second and then the scathing look intensified. "You pinched my ass!"

Justin hooted before he burst ahead of us down the hallway.

"Justin!"

He waved the card in the air. "Good luck getting into the room. I've got the key."

"AH!" And she took off after him.

I stayed back and watched as the two chased each other down the hallway. Justin was laughing, Angie was yelling, but right before she turned the corner, I saw the smile on her face as well. I sighed on the inside. They were in love. They had been for such a long time.

I wanted that. I did, but then an old feeling inside me triggered again.

People didn't find the love they had. Not really. And if they did, they were lucky, incredibly so.

With that thought, I knew I had to get my own room. I was the fifth wheel on this trip. When I went back to the front desk, a worker told me that there were no empty rooms. I needed to have a reservation at least a few weeks in advance. After she told me all this with a blank expression on her face, I wondered if Marissa had booked two rooms from the beginning or even how she got the rooms in the first place.

"Street girl? Alex."

And then I stopped wondering about it.

Cord Tatum stood behind me with his arm around a girl's waist. He was dressed in Grant West University athletic pants and a sweatshirt with the school's crest on it. Two other guys, who were wearing similar outfits, were with him.

His gaze flicked past my shoulder to the front desk worker. "What are you doing? You getting a room?"

"That's cute, thinking you can get a room here." The girl flicked her red hair over her shoulder and laughed. She trailed a hand down his arm and rested it on his chest.

My eyes narrowed at her, but I responded to him, "My friends already got rooms, but they're coupled up. It feels weird, you know?"

"Ah. Got it."

One of the guys nudged him from behind. Cord's eyes lit up. "Hey, we have a few empty beds with the team. You could bunk with one of us. We'd have to put you with a decent guy."

"Or one that's neutered," a buddy snickered behind him.

My smile strained at the corners. "Uh . . ." But I remembered the front desk clerk's snippy words and I drop my bags to the floor. "Sure." I was desperate at that moment. But then I remembered all of his words. "Wait, you said your whole team? Your whole team is staying here?"

He nodded. "Yeah, we have a game tomorrow. I ran into Marissa at the airport and she badgered me for tickets. Said something about her family knowing a travel agent and pulling strings." He shrugged. "It's no big deal. I figured I owed her for what a jackass I was before."

I nodded. I had guessed that was how she'd gotten those tickets, but some excitement sparked in me at the idea of watching

Jesse play again. It'd been too long. It'd been too long since I had felt him, too.

Cord's eyes were thoughtful as he watched my reaction. "I think Hunt got his own room."

The same guy snickered again, "Golden Boy ain't going to share a room, not unless he's banging the chick."

Cord turned on him. "The Golden Boy was best friends with her brother."

His friend's smirk vanished and his eyes widened. The girl straightened and reassessed me. I ignored both of their reactions. "I don't want to bother Jesse. I'm sure he has other things to worry about."

A third guy snorted from the back. "The only thing he's got to worry about is if he gets enough sleep."

Cord's eyes grew hard. "Shut up, Kaseys. We're damn lucky to have Hunt on our team and you know it. He's our best damn player, so show some respect."

The girl had detached herself from his side and migrated closer to me as he had turned toward his buddies. She gave me an intense look now and her voice came out husky, "So you know Jesse Hunt?"

Cord snorted and hauled her back to him. A hand cemented her against his side. "No way, Mel. This girl is off limits."

Her lips stuck out in a pout. "Come on."

"No."

And then one of the guys shouted, "Hunt!"

He was coming in from the sliding doors with a bag over his shoulder. As he looked up, a polite grin was on his face, but then Cord stepped aside and Jesse's eyes landed on me. He froze. I watched with a pounding heart as his hand tightened on his bag strap. "Hey, guys." His eyes zeroed in on me, an unnamed emotion playing just behind his cool façade. "You're here?"

Oh, boy. "Yeah."

He frowned. "But your folks are—"

Cord clapped a hand on his shoulder. "Hey, buddy. So this little beauty here is looking for a room to share. She's here with friends, but they're all coupled up, and the front desk bitch made it clear that there aren't any empty rooms available."

Jesse's eyes had narrowed on me, but he didn't hesitate. "Yeah, she can stay with me."

My heart skipped a beat and I forgot to breathe for a second.

"Sweet. It's all worked out. See you around, Alex." Cord winked at me as he led his friends to the elevator.

Jesse waited until they had gotten into one before he touched my arm. He asked quietly, "You're not here with your parents?"

I shook my head. I couldn't speak.

"They're at The Four Seasons." He had grown so quiet. "You don't want them to know you're here?"

My head wrenched from side to side. I couldn't tell him they had left to escape me. It wouldn't have been fair to them. So, I choked out in a whisper, "They're doing a second honeymoon thing."

"Who did you come with?"

"Marissa and her boyfriend. Angie and Justin."

He settled back. "Got it." His lip twitched at the corner. "Marissa's got another boyfriend? I pity that guy."

"Eric Nathan."

He went still. "What?"

"She's dating Eric Nathan."

His jaw clenched. And then he clipped out, "Good. He's not your problem anymore then."

"Jesse." I sighed.

"Come on." He reached down and grabbed my bag. "I'm tired. We had an early practice and the guys are going out for something to eat if you want to come with."

"You had a practice?" I checked my phone. "At six in the morning?"

Funny. I didn't remember the last time I slept, and yet; I was wired. That wasn't right. It didn't feel right.

He flashed me a grin. "Yeah. And it was at five this morning, but Coach is giving us the day off. We just have to show up for a team dinner tonight and promise that we'll get eight hours of sleep tonight before the game tomorrow." Then he stopped suddenly and turned to face me before he continued. "Your parents are coming to the game tomorrow."

He took a breath.

"My coach knows about Ethan. I've talked to him about it and when he found out that your folks were here . . . they want to do a thing for them during the game.

"There'll be some footage of them, probably just where they are in their seats and they'll dedicate a song in memory of Ethan. I know most people won't care. They're doing it for me too. I think it'll be during halftime or something and they'll do it while other stuff is going on, but I thought you should know. Do you want to go with them? I can get you a ticket."

I shook my head. Everything was so raw now, again. I spoke in a hoarse voice, "Marissa got tickets from Cord, but now I don't know if I should come to the game at all."

His hand grasped my arm. He pulled me close. "I want you to come."

Oh, God. The idea of my parents being there and watching an announcer dedicating something to them . . . pain of a different level flared inside me. I struggled to keep from buckling over and crumbling to the floor. They would announce Ethan's name. I pulled away from Jesse's hand and shook my head. I was so tired of crying, so damn tired. As I swiped some of the cursed tears away, Jesse pulled me back to him. He made a soothing sound as he replaced my hands and wiped them away instead.

More slipped out.

He dried them, too.

And then he glanced up, cursed under his breath, and ripped himself away.

I looked up and into Angie's eyes. Her mouth was open. A strange gurgling sound came out and she pointed a finger toward us. "You . . . you two—what?"

Jesse bent close and whispered in my ear, "Room 2612." Something was pushed into my hand and he stalked away to the elevators.

I glanced down at the key card in my hand. Nothing was making sense again.

Then Angie was at my side and she whispered, "Oh my God."

Oh my God indeed.

The elevator opened and he got on. I yelled out, "Wait!"

The door started to slide closed, but his hand shot out, making the doors slide open again.

When I was sure he wasn't going to leave without me, I turned to Angie. "I'm staying with him."

"What? But—"

I rushed around and hurried to where he was holding the door for me. As I slipped past, he let go of the door and stepped back against that wall. Angie was looking back and forth between us, her mouth hanging open in shock.

I closed my eyes and braced myself. The cat was out of the bag. Angie had suspected, she had approved at first, and then disapproved. Then she forgot, but she was fully reminded now. I knew she thought Jesse had moved on and left me behind, but when she saw the text message he had sent me yesterday, the same disapproval had come back. She hadn't said a word on the airplane or in the taxi, but I knew it was only a matter of time. She was going to question me and she would say the same things I told myself every time.

Jesse was going to hurt me. He already had, but she didn't know that he healed me as well. I needed him, even if it were only in the little increments that I got from him. Because every time, a part of me felt whole, a little more together before he would leave again.

He watched me as I watched her, a grave expression on his face, but neither of us said a word. The air was thick with tension, anticipation, too.

I wanted to be in his arms. I wanted it so badly I could almost taste him.

Then my phone started buzzing. They were text messages from Angie, but I silenced it and put it away.

When the doors slid open on his floor, we walked together to his room. My palms were starting to sweat again. I felt breathless. The door opened and we were inside.

Then I was pulled back. Jesse pushed me against the wall. I had a second to glimpse the lust on his face before his mouth was on mine and I wrapped myself around him.

13

Hours later the sound of someone pounding on the door woke us up. Jesse jerked upright, startled. I flipped to my back and grabbed the blanket to cover me. He grimaced when someone yelled through the door, "Hunt, come on! We're fucking waiting for your ass."

When the unmistakable click of his lock sounded, we both threw ourselves into motion. I grabbed the rest of the blankets and pulled them over my head as Jesse threw himself on the ground for his clothes. Then the door opened, and I cringed. It sounded like more than one guy entered the room. One of them grumbled, "What the hell, Jesse? You take a nap or something?"

"Uh, Reed . . ." a guy cleared his throat.

"Oh, shit!"

"Stop," Jesse barked the last one.

And then there was silence, interrupted by someone snickering, but I let out a breath of relief when I heard all of them leave again. It was so silent for a second that I almost squeaked when someone landed next to me. Still, I didn't make a move. No way. I was sure it was a trick.

"You can come out," Jesse said flatly. "They're outside now."

I poked my head out from the blankets. He grinned at me as he was zipping up his jeans and pulled on a Grant West University sports blazer. Then he disappeared into the bathroom, and I heard water running.

I exhaled. Holy smokes. When the realization of what almost happened settled over me, my arms shook a little. I couldn't believe a bunch of Jesse's teammates had almost seen me naked and in his bed. Well, they did see me in bed but not the naked part. I was hoping Cord and his two friends wouldn't put two and two together, but who was I kidding?

Jesse came back out, a slight whiff of outdoor cologne clung to him; his hair glistening with gel.

Oh dear goodness. I swallowed over a very dry throat again. How was it possible for him to be that dangerously good looking after only five minutes? I wanted to pull him back into bed with me. I licked my lips at the lustful thoughts swirling in my head.

He flashed me a grin before he tossed the same key card from before at me. It landed beside the pile of clothes he had tossed earlier. "I'd invite you to come with, but it's a team thing."

I flashed him a look. Like I would want to have breakfast with all those guys, knowing they knew what I'd been doing an hour before.

"So." My voice was so husky it made me flush in embarrassment.

Jesse smirked.

I tried to clear my throat. "What are you doing for the day?" It didn't work.

He dropped his arms to his sides and straightened from the wall before stalking toward me. My lips were dry again. He got closer. Oh goodness. Slowly, so slowly, he leaned down so his face was inches from mine and both his hands rested on the bed on either side of me. His lips brushed against mine as he spoke, "Lots and lots of sex."

My heart was pounding.

"Really?" I squeaked out.

Then his lips moved into a perfect smile. "What are you doing today?"

"Wha—" But I stopped. I reached up and took hold of the back of his hair.

He tensed, waiting.

I shifted so I was on my knees, and he tried to move back, but my grip on his hair stopped him. The comforter was the only thing that covered me. It was tucked under my arm, but as I lifted myself up and pressed against him, it started to slip. His eyes darkened, but he didn't move. I didn't let him. And then I grinned. My lips brushed against his. His breathing grew shallow, and I felt his heart pick up its pace. It thumped against me as I whispered, caressing him at the same time, "Lots and lots of—"

A pounding on the door stopped me. The same guy yelled through it, "Come on, man! You already banged her. Let's go!"

A mask of fury came over him quickly. He tore himself away from me and was out the door in a second.

"Hey! What the—"

There was a loud crash against the wall. One of the pictures that'd been hanging on the wall crashed to the floor.

"Hey-hey!"

"Hey, man—"

And then someone punched someone.

"Ow!"

"Holy shit!"

"Hey, hey—"

There was more movement in the hallway, more punches were shared, and another crash against the wall.

Jesse's door was slammed shut. It was loud and sudden. I jumped from the tension and staggered to my feet. Hastily, I threw on my clothes, cursing when, in my haste to cover myself, I punched a hole through my sleeve with my thumb. When I pulled my jeans up and my fingers couldn't snap the button, I cursed again and then pushed my hair out of my eyes. I wanted to chop it off at that moment.

I couldn't let him get hurt, not because of me.

I reached for the handle, ready to yank it open when a loud voice boomed outside. "What THE HELL is going on out here?"

All the fighting stopped.

"Hey, Coach." a voice strangled out.

"Hunt?"

"Yeah, Coach?"

I heard the hostility that was still in Jesse's voice.

"Camden?"

A grunt was his response.

"You two, in Hunt's room. Now."

I sucked in my breath.

"Uh, Coach—"

"Now!" he barked.

I heard Jesse's groan and grabbed my bag. Then I looked for a hiding spot. What the hell was I doing? I had no idea, but this was beyond embarrassing. I snatched my bra from the dresser and threw myself into the closet just as the door opened again.

I could see through the crack between the doors. Jesse was the first one in. He paused as he scanned the room, then he hesitated to go farther in.

"Hunt, let's go." The impatience from his coach was evident. "We don't have all day and I don't want my two best shooters to be fighting. I want this fixed and I want it done now. Camden, sit your ass down."

He grunted again and passed Jesse.

I couldn't see where they all sat, but Jesse stood by the counter. I could see him clearly and knew that he kept glancing toward the bathroom.

"Okay." The coach let out a deep sigh. "What the hell is going on between you two?"

"Coach, he came out of nowhere—"

"Don't give me that bullshit, Camden. I heard what you said to him. My room's across the hall, and if I had a girl I cared about and you said the same thing, I'd beat the shit out of you, too. This has been going on for a while. I want it dealt with, now."

Jesse's shoulders dropped down. He sounded regretful. "He's got a problem with me—"

"He's a fucking freshman, and he acts as if he's the entire team, Coach." Camden was on his feet now. I saw his shadow grow in size. "I'm the captain. I call the shots—"

"*I* call the shots. Now sit, Camden."

He didn't.

The coach stood, and his tone took on an authoritative tone that made me grip my bag tighter. "You will sit now, Camden. Now!"

He sat.

I almost sat.

He let loose with a string of curses. "I can't believe my two best are pulling this shit now. Now! We have a big game tomorrow. We're in Las Vegas and the two of you are trading punches in the damn hallway like teenagers who learned what their penises are for. Have you gone nuts? Are you high?" He shot a hand out. "Don't even answer that. I don't want to touch that with a ten foot pole."

Jesse spoke softly, "We're not doing drugs, Coach."

"Then what the hell is going on?"

"He's threatened by me."

There was no ego attached to the accusation, and the simplicity of it had the rest of the room in silence.

"Camden?"

There was no response.

The coach prodded again, "Is that true?"

Then a fourth guy cleared his throat. "Walt, we should get going. We've probably missed our reservation anyway, but the rest of the guys are waiting outside. These two idiots can fix this later tonight."

"Yeah, you're right." But the coach didn't sound as if he was sure of it. Then he grunted, "Camden, if that's true, that you're doing all this shit because you're threatened, then you aren't the captain I thought you were. Straighten it up, lead the team, and leave your damn ego courtside. I don't want this affecting us tomorrow."

There was a series of soft curses before Coach spoke again, "And Hunt?"

Jesse straightened.

"Keep doing what you do. You keep your head screwed on right. You play every time with the same consistency, and when you're riled up, you dominate everybody. You hear that, Camden? This 'freshman' can't be beat when he's pissed off. You really want to play that card with him? You the captain or not?"

There was silence.

"I didn't hear you, Camden!" the coach roared. "You the captain or not?"

"Yes, sir."

"Do you lead this team?"

"Yes, sir!"

"Then lead it. It's not going to be the first time you run against someone better than you are. It's how you handle it that'll determine your future. Just don't fuck it up when you're on my team, you hear me?"

"Yes, sir!"

"Yes, sir what?"

"Yes, sir, Coach!"

He grunted in approval and passed the closet for the door. He stopped so close to the door that I closed my eyes. I could've pissed my pants at that moment.

"And Hunt?"

"Yeah, Coach?"

"Get the girl out of the closet."

It wasn't long before the door slammed shut again. Everything on the wall and closet doors rattled from the strength of it.

Someone walked to the closet door, but I heard Jesse growl, "Reed, touch it and die."

The doors swished open. I found myself staring at a tall guy, lean build, with striking blue eyes and blonde hair. He was dressed similar to Jesse. He frowned at me, but offered his hand. "I'm sorry. I didn't mean any disrespect to you. Reed Camden."

I couldn't move. I couldn't breathe. I certainly couldn't shake his hand. *He looked exactly like Ethan.*

I bent over. I *really* couldn't breathe. I started to wheeze.

"Hey!"

Gentle hands touched my shoulders. I bent my head between my knees and gasped for breath. I couldn't—I couldn't even see. "Jesse."

"I'm here." He lifted me out of the closet and carried me to the bed. As he sat, I curled into him.

"Dude, what the hell?"

"Just go with the team. I won't make it."

"What's wrong with her?"

My hands grabbed on to Jesse's blazer, and I pressed into him. His hands rubbed down my back in soothing motions the whole time. Oh God. He looked so much like Ethan, *too* much like him.

"Jesse," I whimpered.

I felt him press a kiss to my shoulder and then he hissed, "Fucking go, Reed!"

I trembled in Jesse's arms.

He cursed under his breath and readjusted his hold on me. His arms were more secure around me.

Reed went to the door, but he returned again. He sat on the other bed with a fierce frown. "What's wrong with her?"

Jesse shook his head and cursed at him. "This is when you decide to be friendly?"

He shrugged. His voice came out wrangled. "My sister has night terrors. This hits home with me."

"Oh, God." The disgust was evident with Jesse, but he lifted me on his lap again. This time, he propped me up and smoothed my hair away from my forehead. His tone gentled. "Hey, hey. Come on. Look at me. Please stop crying, Alex."

His desperation did the deed, and I swallowed all the pain away. He needed me. I might've been losing it, but I knew that Jesse was on the verge as well. He needed me to come back and be the strong one. My hand slipped into his as I took gulping breaths to stuff my hysteria down.

The guy looked like him. So what?

There were lots of guys that looked like Ethan, but then I looked at him again. Everything stopped in me. Oh God. He was the spitting image of him. How could this be? How could there be another Ethan in the world?

"Hey, hey." Jesse sat me up even more and ran his hand up and down my back in a brisk motion. "Come on. Breathe, Alex. Breathe."

I breathed. Then I gulped for more air.

"You want me to call Angie?"

I shook my head. Some tears slipped down my cheek, but I ignored them. I had to deal with it. It was about time I started dealing with it. But I couldn't look away from the guy's piercing eyes. Someone stabbed me in the gut. And then someone reached inside me, took hold of my heart, and ripped it out. I felt like my heart was beating in a stranger's hands and I was staring at it. The trembling started in. Jesse cursed again, but lifted me in his arms.

"Jesse!"

"This is enough." The resolve on his face made me pause. It was set and determined. He was tired, hell, he was exhausted as he carried me into the bathroom, turned the shower on full blast, and dumped me into the tub.

I screamed.

"Dude!"

Jesse held Reed back. Jesse's eyes caught mine as I gasped against the onslaught of cold water. I couldn't look away. There was a fevered determination in him, and I knew he'd had enough. It was time to stop.

I stood then. Something centered in me that I hadn't felt in a long time, maybe ever. Ethan was with us in the room right then. I felt him, and the hairs on the back of my neck stood upright.

Jesse's eyes blinked rapidly. His face faltered for a second. I knew he felt him, too. But then his impassive mask slipped back into place. His eyes bored me down, and he leaned against the doorframe. His captain was behind him with an expression akin to surprise and amazement on his face.

I rasped out, "He's here."

Jesse nodded. The wall was back in place. I couldn't reach him, but I wanted to. I needed to.

As I stood in the tub with the cold water beating down on me, shivers wracked through me. Goose bumps ran up and down my arms and legs. Ethan was dead, but his memory felt so alive. I jerked my eyes to Jesse's captain. He paled, but he didn't look away. Then I held my hand out.

He looked at it strangely.

Jesse moved aside, and Reed stepped forward. He shook my hand.

"Thank you. It's nice to meet you."

His eyes were wide as he looked from me to Jesse and back, but his hand squeezed around mine. "Thanks. You, too."

He pulled his hand back and retreated into the hallway. "I'll—um—I'll see you later, Hunt."

Jesse didn't blink an eye or react when the door slammed closed. But he gave me a sad smile. "Are you okay?"

I nodded. "I think I will be." And I meant it.

14

Jesse refused to leave for his team's breakfast until he was sure I would be fine. I was warm. I was dressed. And I was hungry. An hour after he left, I made my way through the hallways to the room Angie had texted was theirs. I was emotionally exhausted. Seeing Ethan's look-alike had sent me reeling. I hadn't expected it, but I was back to being okay.

I couldn't explain what had been shared between Jesse and me, but I felt stronger because of it. I couldn't keep crying. I couldn't keep breaking down. It was time to start thinking of Ethan in a different way. I decided that when I felt him around me, I wasn't going to be scared anymore.

Then I took a deep breath and ran my hands down my pants. My stomach was all twisted inside, but it was time to be strong again. It'd been so long. And then I stopped outside of Angie's door. A completely different storm started inside me. This was it. She knew about Jesse and me. Well, she'd always known, but she had assumed it had stopped and I'd never corrected her. I knew she'd be disappointed in me. Angie felt a girl should only sleep with a guy if they're committed and in love. I loved Jesse, but I knew better to expect reciprocated feelings or commitment. When I was stronger, when I could bear the idea of losing him, I'd walk away. I only hoped I wouldn't be too shattered at that point. I raised my hand and knocked.

It was time.

She opened the door and didn't disguise her anger at all. Her shoulders were rigid and her eyes were hard. With a gesture inside, she murmured, "Let's talk."

Oh boy.

Marissa was on the dresser. Her legs were dangling, and she was twiddling her thumbs in her lap. When she looked up, she bit her lip and looked back down. When I perched on the end of the bed, Angie stood beside her. She crossed her arms and raised her chin. Marissa didn't look back up, but that didn't matter.

Angie started. "So?"

"So?"

She rolled her eyes. "Are you going to explain it now?"

"Explain what?"

"Jesse Hunt!" Her arms went wide. "My God, you left with him. You haven't been answering your phone. I mean, what is going on with you two?"

A spark of anger lit in me. "You knew about us. You've known since August. You just assumed that he would've forgotten me, didn't you?"

"I . . ." She sighed. Her mouth opened and then closed a few times before she managed to say anything more. "I don't know what I thought. Yes, I thought it stopped with you two. He's going to destroy you. Don't you see that? Can't you stop it?"

My blank face was my response. It was none of her business. Her opinions had been heard, but it didn't stop me. It wasn't going to stop me. Seeing that, she threw her hands in the air again. Then she twisted to the side. "Marissa? Don't you have anything to say?"

She glanced up and gave a shrug. "Um, I don't feel like I have anything worthwhile to share."

"Are you kidding me?"

"What do you want me to say? She's going to do what she wants to do. I mean, we've told her our worries, but that's all we can do. We can't make her not see him." Then she bit her lip again and looked down. Her thumbs were twiddling a second later.

"Oh my God! I can't believe the two of you." Angie jerked to me again. "You don't have anything else to say?"

I kept my voice calm. "I've never lied to you, not openly. I might not have shared certain information with you, but I never really lied to you. You guys knew about Jesse. I just didn't tell you that it hadn't stopped when I realized you thought it had."

"But, there." Her arm shot at me, pointing. "Right there is a lie. You lied to me by not correcting me. I'm your friend, Alex. Why wouldn't you share this with me?"

"Because of this. You don't like him—"

"That's not true."

"—you don't like the idea of him and me—"

"That's true."

"—and you're only saying all this stuff because you think there's no chance that Jesse would ever be with me." I finished out of breath. My chest was heaving.

Her mouth twisted into a frown. "I didn't, that's not all true."

"Yes, it is," Marissa spoke up timidly.

"What?" Angie whirled around to face her. Her arms got tighter over her chest. "You agree with her?"

"Just that . . ." She stopped, pale in her face. Then she looked away, shrugging once again. "Never mind."

My mouth dropped open.

Angie's eyebrows went high. "What? No, what? What were you going to say?"

"Nothing," she mumbled.

"Marissa." Her voice was harsh. "Come on. You just agreed with everything I said this morning, and now you're backing down? You don't agree with me? I look like a fool."

I frowned, but Marissa's head shot back up. "That's not true, and it's not about you. You have an opinion on her life, but you're forgetting that we're not all as *perfect* as you."

"I agree."

Angie shot me a glare but turned back to her. "Excuse me?"

Marissa visibly swallowed and tucked her hands under her legs. Then she looked up, a brave front. "You forget that some of us don't have the perfect boyfriend. We don't have the perfect relationship. We're not you. We're not as lucky as you are."

Angie's mouth dropped to the ground. She was speechless. Then she gurgled out, "Are you kidding me?"

She was right. Marissa was totally right, but when Angie swung her fierce gaze toward me, I looked down. I had escaped the lion's den so far, and I sent a mental thank you to Marissa. However, a different tension filled the room now. Angie had been called out on something she didn't want to hear, even I knew that much. The question was, how was she going to take it?

"You are so stupid!"

Not well.

"Excuse me?" Marissa's eyes flashed from anger. She sat like a queen now. There was no slouch at all in her posture.

"I can't believe you. You don't have any idea of what you're talking about."

"Yes, I do," Marissa cried out. She was heated. "You're so goddamn perfect all the time, Angie. None of us can measure up to you. And so what if Jesse and Alex are screwing around? If I did that with him, you wouldn't care. You'd pester me for details and you'd even get excited, but you'd laugh at me behind my back. I know how you operate, Angie. Me, I'm just some stupid slut, but Alex, heavens no. She's a saint to you. Wake up! She's a mess. She has been since her brother died. I'm not surprised at all that she screwing him. He's hot."

A grin broke free from me. I couldn't hold it back.

Angie snorted from disgust and blasted both of us with her frosty glare. "I can't believe either of you two. You both are settling, and I think it's revolting. I don't want my friends to settle for less than what they deserve. You deserve a guy who loves you. You deserve a guy who'll be open and honest about how he feels about you."

She stopped suddenly. Her shallow breaths were loud in the quiet room, but then Marissa hopped to her feet. Her chin was set, and she flared in defiance. "I don't care what you say. You don't know me anymore, Ang. You used to, but some messed up crap has happened to me. You have no idea, and you have no right to judge me. I won't stick around for it."

"But—" Angie's mouth dropped once again. When she saw that Marissa was about to leave, her long finger extended toward me. "We're here for *her*, not for you and me. You called me, remember? You were the one who said we needed to get Alex out of the house and have a trip. What the hell? How did we get into a fight? This was all about Alex."

I straightened at that. "Excuse me?"

Her mouth snapped back shut. "Nothing."

My gaze whipped to Marissa. "What is she talking about?"

Her eyes were wide, fearful, but then she crumbled. She said so quietly, "I saw your parents at the airport, Alex."

Nothing. I felt nothing.

There was no friendliness. There was no warmth. There wasn't even pain. I'd gone numb again. "And?" I needed to hear it all, and from the torment on her face, I knew there was a bunch more.

I got myself ready.

"We know they ditched you for the holidays."

Oh. They knew.

"Well?" Both of them watched me.

"What?"

"That's it? That's all you're going to say?" Angie seemed dumbfounded.

I shrugged. "What do you want me to say? You already knew."

"But they're here," she cried out. "They're here to see Jesse, and they're not including you in anything."

"They're married. That's for them to do. This is like a second honeymoon or something."

Her arms flung wide again. "I would be going crazy. I would be calling them and chewing them out. How dare they forget you! You're their child. You're their only kid alive. You'd think they'd go overboard with you since they lost Ethan."

Pain ripped through me. A shudder of torment that I'd always suppressed broke free at hearing those words. They'd been thoughts that I had over the past year, but I'd never voiced them. I never said a word to my parents. They were grieving. They had lost Ethan, too. So I gave them their distance. I became the good girl for them. I didn't want them to have to worry about me, but then it had gone too far. They stopped caring. They stopped loving. It felt as if I wasn't their child anymore. They had always loved Ethan more, but after this year, I was starting to wonder if they had ever loved me.

I didn't want to burden them. I didn't want to *be* a burden to them. It was best to remain quiet.

I shrugged again, but I couldn't look at them. It hurt too much, and I didn't want them to see that. "Its fine, you guys."

"It's not!"

Then I gave up and surrendered. "What are you going to do about it?"

They stopped. They blinked. Their mouths opened. No sound came out. They were like owls. After a while, Angie strangled out, "What do you mean?"

"What do you want me to do?"

"I . . ." She closed her mouth again. There was nothing.

"Exactly." And for the first time, I let my pain shine through. I couldn't hold it back. I didn't want to anymore. Maybe it was because I was finally hearing someone defend me or support me, but I stopped hiding that pain. And I knew the instant they both saw it, because they gasped.

"Alex," Angie whispered.

Marissa wrenched away. Her arms folded around herself.

"Are you going to reprimand my parents for not loving me as much anymore?" Those damn tears started coming again. I barely felt them as I whispered more, "Are you going to tell my mom that she was selfish when she tried to kill herself? Or tell my dad that he shouldn't have to only worry about his wife, but his daughter, too? They're both grieving, Ang. We're all still grieving."

Suddenly, Marissa took off. The door slammed behind her.

"What?" Angie shrieked again. Her stricken eyes skirted from the door to me. "What the hell was that?"

It should've hurt that she had left, but it barely fazed me. She was the least of my problems.

"I can't believe—Alex, what do I do here?"

I shrugged. They opened this can of worms. She should deal with it, but then I stood and brushed away the wetness on my cheeks. I was so tired of it all. "I'm going to go."

"No, please."

"Angie."

"What?" She had conflicting emotions on her face. Concern, anger, and another unnamed one flitted over her. Then she shook her head and grabbed my arm. Her fingers wrapped tightly around it. "What do I do here? I have no idea. And what the hell happened with Marissa?"

"You do nothing. It's not the first time when things got too real and someone bailed."

Her fingers jerked in reaction. "That's happened to you before, huh?"

"More than you want to know."

My friend looked like the world had just beaten her at her own game. I swallowed all my pain down and patted her hand. "Why don't you find Justin? I'm hungry. We could get something to eat together?"

She blinked back some tears of her own. "What about Jesse?"

I shrugged. "I'm here with you guys."

"Really?" Some hope sparked back to her. "I'm sorry for pushing you. That was the intent, Alex. It really was. Marissa called and told me your parents ditched you, we were both so mad. I didn't think about it, not really. She said she had the rooms already booked, and I didn't think about that either. I grabbed Justin and told him where we were going." She sighed. A dreamy smile came over her. "He never questioned me or anything. He's such a great guy. I'm lucky to have him. I really am."

I nudged her toward the door. "Go get your dreamboat. I'll meet you guys in the lobby."

She skidded to a halt before the door and fixed me with a stare. "Are you sure you're okay?"

"I will be." The concern still lingered so I fixed a bright smile on my face. It blasted her. "I promise."

Sadness filled her eyes, but she nodded. "You're lying to me, but that's okay. I'm going to be there for you no matter what, even if stupid and hot Jesse Hunt destroys you. I'll be there."

"You have to, Marissa just bolted."

She grimaced. "Don't remind me. I'm going to have a word with her later about that, too."

I grinned, but I knew I didn't want to be in the room when that happened. I was about to ask her to give me a heads up when she was going to approach that topic with Marissa, but there was a knock at the door. Angie opened it, revealing Justin and Eric standing in the hallway.

"Where's Marissa?" Eric peered past our shoulders.

"Your girlfriend ditched. No idea where she is or when she's coming back," Angie snapped out. Her eyes flashed in anger.

Justin went into action. He threw his arms around his girlfriend, pulled her in close, and nuzzled her neck as he rocked her back and forth in his arms.

"Justin!"

He ignored her weak attempts at swatting his head and winked at me. "I'm starving, honey. I'm ravenous. I'm about to faint in the hallway. My stomach needs food, woman. It needs sustenance. I can't handle this anymore." And then he let loose and belted out, "I don't need no more pain, no more game, no more drama."

As he kept singing, Angie smacked his shoulder and pulled out of his hold. "My boyfriend is a freak show. I can't take him anywhere." She muttered under her breath as she stalked past him.

Justin watched her go with a wide smile on his face, and then he raced to catch up. The two were giggling together soon after and chased each other up and down the hallway.

"So, Marissa took off?" Eric smiled at me, tentatively.

Oh right. I'd forgotten he was there. Let the awkwardness ensue. He had wanted to date me, I evaded him, so he was with the girl that had just ditched him. I kept my voice light. "Yeah, but don't worry. She's like that when things hit close to home with her. She'll show up again."

His shoulders didn't relax.

I didn't care.

"She's upset about something."

No shit, Sherlock. But I held my tongue. "She'll come around. She always does."

At the second reassurance, his shoulders sagged and he nodded. Some of the tension left him. "You're right. She does."

If Angie had been there, she would've warned him that

Marissa would probably show up with another guy wrapped around her. I wasn't like Angie, though. I held my tongue and didn't say a word. He needed to learn. He would. Marissa always showed her true colors when it came to guys. They either cheated on her or she cheated on them. It wasn't something we talked about or questioned her about, but it'd been happening more and more the past two years. If I had been half the friend to Marissa that Angie was to me, I would have stepped in. I wasn't. I couldn't ignore the fact that I was still mad at her for all her betrayals, for going after Jesse, and then going after Eric. She had helped me avoid his attempts, but she hadn't asked. She hadn't cared. She picked him and she went after him.

As we continued to the lobby where Angie and Justin were waiting, I also admitted to myself the other side of the coin. I might've dated Eric. I might've finally listened to my head and tried to move on from Jesse. Eric might've helped me avoid the disaster that Angie knew was coming later, but he was with Marissa now. And he was going to get his own heart shattered by her.

There was no sympathy inside me for him. We were both going to get hurt.

15

W e didn't hear from Marissa until later that night. I didn't hear from Jesse either, so I assumed that meant he didn't want to hang out either. After we ate, we spent the rest of the afternoon at the pool. Justin disappeared at one part of the afternoon. He came back a few hours later with fake licenses for us. Angie's eyes went wide, but she took hers without a comment. Praise the Lord. When I took mine, there was a dip in my stomach. I knew I shouldn't feel guilty. This wasn't the right thing to do, but we were in Vegas. My parents had ditched me. One of my best friends had ditched me. The guy I loved, but couldn't really have, had ditched me for the day.

I took the card and shoved all the other crap away. I wanted to have fun and those thoughts would only get in the way.

Eric was more excited when he got his. He'd been quiet most of the afternoon, but a cocky look came over him then.

Angie whipped around to look at me. Yep, she saw it, too. I shrugged at the look, but good for him. Maybe I didn't want him to wait around for the inevitable Marissa break-up scene? I had no idea, but when the four of us got ready to go out, I was determined to have a good time.

Angie giggled as she came into the bathroom with her makeup bag. "I can't believe we snuck your bag out of Jesse's room."

I grinned at her in the mirror, but a pang of regret sliced through me. Since Marissa was still missing and there'd been no word from Jesse, we had decided the four of us would go out to the clubs that night. Even though I hadn't considered my sleeping arrangements that night, I wanted to get ready with Angie. The guys were in Eric's room doing whatever they did.

I replied as I steadied my eyeliner, "I needed my things." And that was it. That was the end of the story.

"So where do you think Marissa is?"

I shrugged. I didn't even want to think about her.

Her voice dropped as she asked, "Do you think she's trying to get together with Cord again?"

I dropped the eyeliner and turned, suddenly breathless. Marissa and Cord. That meant she was around Jesse, whom I hadn't heard from all day. I gulped. But then I stopped again. He wasn't my boyfriend. He wasn't my anything. He was my brother's best friend, my *dead* brother's best friend. I tried to convince myself that was all we were, but I couldn't. I couldn't lie to myself. It hurt that he hadn't texted me all day, but I also knew I was being unreasonable. He was in Vegas for his team, for their game. Not for me.

"I don't know, but I can see her trying something again with him."

"Whatever happened with them? I thought the two of them were perfect for each other." Angie giggled again as she went to the room and reappeared with a full glass, which I eyed suspiciously. "What? We're in Vegas. Aren't we supposed to drink?"

"Where's mine?"

Delight flashed over her face before she disappeared for a second. Then she came back with my own glass filled to the brim.

"Cheers, Alex." She lifted her wine in the air. "Here's to us, to having a great time no matter what drama happens, and to our friendship."

"To us." My glass clinked with hers, "And to having a mother-fucking great time."

More giggles burst from her, but we drank half our glasses.

Then she grew silent for a second.

My glass went to the counter. I knew what this was; this was the pre-air of silence. This was when she was thoughtful as a sudden idea came to her. The next stage was her pursed lips, which I saw just happened. Then she would frown and glance at me; she did both again. Then she'd bite her lip. Yep, once again I was right on cue. The last step was when she'd take a deep breath, readying herself for whatever she was going to say. And, dread filled me when I saw her take that deep breath. It was deeper than normal . . . and we had blast off.

"So, if Marissa hooks up with Cord again, then she and Eric are done." Angie's eyes were filled with concern. "What are you going to do if he wants to date you again? Because I know he hasn't stopped liking you. He just went with Marissa because she was giving him all the signs and well, you know why."

If Marissa liked a guy, she chased him down.

I shrugged and took a deep breath.

"What are you going to do, Alex?" She edged closer, dropping her voice to a whisper. "Would you date him? I mean, I know you have this thing with Jesse, but come on. He's not going to date you, not for real. You know that."

I did know that.

"You're better off with Eric. I think you should make a move on him tonight."

"He's still dating Marissa," I hissed at her.

She was the nonchalant one now. "We both know that's going to end tonight. It's just a question of who Marissa's with now. I bet you money that she already tried to throw herself at Cord. I don't know what happened, but I know he walked away from her. I'm right, aren't I?"

Her eyes were steadily on mine in the mirror.

"I know you know." She said it so faint, I might've imagined it. But I hadn't. "It's okay, you know. You kept that a secret for her. You're a good friend to her."

Oh boy. "Angie."

"It's fine. It really is." She grabbed her glass and drank the rest of the wine. Then she cleared her throat, looking anywhere but at me. "She's a horrible friend to you and you're a great one back to her. And me, I'm a great friend to you and all you do is keep secrets from me. It hurts, Alex, but it's fine. I should expect this, you know."

I heard the change in her tone and stiffened. A different sense of dread took root in me.

"It was always the two of you before. You were both the party girls. Cute, little. All the guys loved you two, especially when you were drinking, but then Ethan died and you became a ghost of what you were. Marissa stepped back, you know, and me . . ." She gulped with tears in her eyes, "I was there for you. I have been there for you. I've tried, Alex. I really have, but you two still have each other's backs. I don't get it. I really don't."

"Angie."

"I don't think I'll ever get it."

"Angie." She was about to leave the bathroom again, but I grabbed her arm. "It's not like that."

"Then what is it like? I really want to understand. Maybe then it won't hurt so goddamn much." Her voice had dropped to a hoarse whisper at the end.

I flinched. I hadn't realized I'd been hurting her, but then I took a deep breath. "You have loving parents."

"So? That means I can't be in your little club because my parents love me?"

"No, that's not what I'm saying. I'm saying that you might not understand because your parents love you. You have a boyfriend who loves you. You don't get the other side, of when parents don't love you or don't treat you how you should be treated. Your parents protect you. They care about you, look over you. Mine stopped a long time ago." I swallowed more pain away and confessed, "They stopped even before Ethan died." It was why I had been partying so much.

"So what? I don't get it."

"I don't cover for Marissa because I know all her secrets, but because I can guess at some of them. I have no idea what's happened to her, but something did. She wouldn't go through guys like she does if she had parents like yours."

"Pat and Lorna are not like that. They're good parents. They love her. They're best friends with mine—"

"I know." I gentled my tone. "They're your parents' best friends, but not all households are like yours. And I'm not even saying it has to do with them. I'm saying that something happened to Marissa. She hasn't been the same Marissa since eighth grade. She changed that year, remember?"

Her eyes hollowed out and I knew she was remembering that year.

"She didn't come to school the same."

Angie nodded, biting her lip. "I know. She was so different."

"But remember at the beginning? She was quiet all the time, not the normal Marissa. Then suddenly she started hanging out with the older group?"

"She started dating Chad Lowerster." Her nose wrinkled up. "He was so gross."

"Gross to us, but hot to her. He was a sophomore. Marissa was in eighth grade."

She rolled her eyes. "I never understood why she was dating him. It was obvious he only wanted one thing."

I remembered how excited she'd been and how disgusted Angie had been. I sobered at the memory. It'd been the first sign that something was wrong. The Marissa before would've been revolted at the idea of dating someone like Chad Lowerster, but then she started openly chasing guys like him. I started to say something about how we needed to be better friends to her, but my phone's alert went off. A tingle raced through me. It was from Jesse; I knew it before looking.

Angie mused as she inspected her teeth in the mirror, "You think we should say something to her about that?"

The phone needed to wait a minute. "About what?"

She lifted an easy shoulder. "I don't know, maybe about how she jumps from guy to guy? She was all about saying something to you, but bailed when you came into the room. You think she wants us to say something to her?"

Had I wanted them to say something? That wasn't the real question. Had I wanted someone to find out about my family? They still didn't know the extent of it, Jesse didn't either. So, I shook my head. "I have no idea. I really don't."

"Hmmm." Then she dropped her hands and turned with a bright smile. "Okay, no more dramatics. You ready to have some fun tonight?"

Was I? My phone's alert went off again. "You bet!"

She beamed back at me.

It wasn't until later as we had met the guys in the hallway and were walking toward the lounge that I snuck a peek at my phone. However, Eric sidled up next to me with a strange glint in his eyes. He lifted a hand to run it through his hair, messing it up, but the look suited him. It gave him a rakish appeal that I knew most girls would swoon over. He wore a black shirt that molded to his frame with low-riding jeans. He could've been a model in that outfit, a thought that I'd never had about him before. But his eyes had been dark as they'd trailed up and down me when we first stepped into the hallway. They were still darkened in lust now.

"You think we'll see Marissa before the trip's over?" he asked.

I started to shrug, but stopped. I told him the truth. "Yes, we'll see her when she decides to show up."

"And she'll be with another guy."

It wasn't a question any longer. He already knew.

"I'm sorry, Eric." But I wasn't. And from the clenching in his jaw, I knew he knew it as well.

But then he changed the topic and forced a light cheery note in his voice. "You look sexy tonight."

He skimmed me up and down again. To my surprise, a shiver followed his gaze over my body.

Angie threw me a wink over her shoulder. She was the proud momma, since she had argued with me about my attire that night for twenty minutes. In the end, I succumbed and wore the black dress that draped over my breasts and down to my hips. My entire back was exposed, along with the sides of my hips. It ended a few inches above my knees, but for some reason I didn't feel embarrassed. I would've a month ago.

"You can thank Angie."

She grinned and giggled, but Justin's hand was on the small of her back. His fingers flexed in a possessive hold as he gave her a wolf whistle. "Eric, I like you, man, but you better not comment on my woman."

"Noted."

"Good."

The two shared a smirk as we came to the elevators.

Angie rolled her eyes at me, and I grinned, but then the doors slid open and everything stopped.

Jesse stared back at me. His eyes widened as he took in my dress, but then he was jostled forward as his teammates pushed him out the door. Cord whistled at me, "Looking good, Street Girl."

"Street girl?" Angie threw me a frown.

Then Camden stepped around Jesse and threw his hand out.

"Can I please meet you again? Hunt, tell me we're hanging out with your girl tonight? Please, tell me we are."

Another guy snickered, "This the girl who was hiding in the closet? I wish I'd stuck around."

"Yeah, right. You pissed your pants when coach came out in the hallway."

"Shut up, Wiscers."

"You shut up, pussy."

Jesse stepped closer as Justin threw his hand out. "Thanks, man, for the IDs."

I did the double take now. "You got them for us?"

Jesse shrugged. "Who else do you guys know here?"

Angie was transfixed by one of the guys, and I saw her mouth the word, "closet" before she narrowed her eyes at me.

"Nathan." Jesse gave him a brisk nod.

Eric, who had stiffened at the sight of him, gave him the same gesture. "Hunt."

Then Jesse turned his back on him and faced me. It was smoothly and perfectly done, and it was more effective because of it. He'd cut him out of the conversation. I knew Eric registered the insult when his jaw clenched, but he didn't combat it. He even stepped farther back.

"I texted you." He dropped his voice so only I could hear him. His fingers touched my arm and he urged me back, away from the group. "Where are you guys going tonight?"

I had read the two messages quickly, but that was when Eric had approached me. I hadn't had time to really think about what he had asked. "You knew we were going out tonight?"

"Yeah, I figured. Houston reached out to me about the fakes this afternoon. I can't go out late tonight, but I thought I'd come for a while."

I blinked at all that information. So he'd known where I was the whole time, who I was with. "That's why you didn't text me today."

"You were with your friends."

"And you didn't want to pull me away from them?"

He gave me a wolfish grin. "If I had, you know what we'd be doing all day."

Another shiver wracked through my body, one that had my every cell tingling in anticipation. I almost groaned from the dark thoughts that were going on in my mind, but bit my lip and held it back. My voice came out husky, "Jesse."

His finger was rubbing up and down my arm. He grinned at the torment he was causing and slipped an arm around my waist to pull me close. As he bent close, I closed my eyes. I could feel his breath against my skin and waited for the feel of his lips, but then Angie's voice came out loud. "Are you ready, Alex?"

Jesse froze and then hissed through his teeth. He pulled away. I caught the dark look he gave my best friend, but then he released me and stepped away. The effort seemed to cost him, but he just kept glaring. "Really, Russo?"

A heated look flashed in her eyes as she raised her chin in the air. "Really, Hunt."

A different promise was smoldering in his depths.

Justin watched the exchange, but moved away from Angie's hold. "You coming with us, Hunt?"

"Justin," she hissed.

He ignored her. "We're going to some clubs. The girls wanted to dance."

Camden had been quiet, but he cleared his throat now. "Most of the team is going to Haze for a couple hours, but we can't be out late. We have our game tomorrow."

Another guy spoke up, "Yeah, if we don't get a full eight hours of sleep, Coach will kill us."

"We wouldn't want to trouble you guys. I'm sure you have all sorts of tramps to hang out with."

"Angie." I glared at her.

She shrugged. "Really."

Camden had been frowning at her when he caught the glare Jesse sent her way. He stepped forward again. "That's no problem. We have a reservation and everything. No waiting line. Some private dancing area all to yourselves. I know they tend to cater to the girls, too, but if you don't want to go there with us, that's no problem."

Angie's smile turned frosty, the heat increasing in her eyes.

Justin coughed as he turned away from her. "Yeah, man. We're all for it."

"Justin," she hissed again and tried to grab for him.

He evaded her reach easily. "I don't suppose you guys are ready to go?"

Jesse, who had fallen silent, spoke first, "We're ready."

"Oh, great," my best friend muttered. Everyone heard, but no one responded.

As we all got into the elevator, I was tense. Jesse's teammates were in a good mood, as was Justin, but Eric and Angie were both glowering in silence. Then, I glanced up and caught Jesse's gaze. He winked at me, and I wasn't so tense anymore either.

16

As we entered the club, a hostess met us at the door. She had perfect teeth, bleached blonde hair, and wore a skimpy uniform. Her eyes trailed over the group and lingered on Jesse, who stood next to me. He had a hand on the small of my back, but straightened as she headed straight for him. Her arm was extended. "Jesse Hunt! Welcome to Haze! It's a pleasure to have you here."

Then she trailed over the group again. Her eyes lingered on me, but her smile never slipped. "We were not aware you were with the Grant West group. We'll make the accommodations immediately. Will your father be joining you?"

He straightened abruptly. The easy smile he'd had vanished. A hard look came over him. "He's here?"

Her eyes widened a fraction. "He was in earlier, I believe." She was rattled from the sudden intensity from him; hell, I was as well. She still oozed a professional friendliness that verged on the line of being too friendly.

"Hunt, I didn't know your dad was coming to our game." Camden pushed through the crowd and slapped a hand on his shoulder.

The hostess' eyes skipped over him, but snapped back to Jesse.

My eyes had narrowed as I watched the exchange and I saw the interest in her depths. I couldn't blame her. Jesse was hot when he was laidback, but he was lethal when he was angry, which he certainly was now. His eyes were hard, jaw clenched, and his body had tensed. A dangerous aura came off him in waves.

And then Angie pushed forward. She gave the hostess a chilly smile. "Can we please go to whatever these guys booked? I have to pee and I don't think you want me to take a piss on your floor. Or would you like to gawk at the famous movie director's son some more?"

The guys snickered and Camden was taken aback. He rapidly glanced from Angie to Jesse, who had shifted closer to me again.

The hostess returned Angie's chilly smile before she turned. "Follow me, gentlemen."

Angie huffed, but no one paid her any attention. Justin curled his arm around her waist and drew her close again.

We were taken to a private box on the second floor, overlooking the dancing area. Camden threw his arm up and gestured around the table. "Can we get a round of shots, on me?"

The hostess glanced at Jesse, who murmured, "We'll take the VIP treatment."

Her smile was blinding before she left.

"Dude, what was that?"

Jesse stiffened beside me. "Nothing. We're going to get our own bottles and shit."

A guy snorted from across the table. "Coach is going to kill us if we're all hungover."

"Yeah." Camden frowned. "We should take it easy tonight, party tomorrow night."

"I know." Jesse's eyes had remained hard at the mention of his father, but they slipped another notch into the danger area as he stared his captain down. Camden glanced at me, then lowered his eyes, and turned to one of his friends.

"Street girl." Cord tapped me on the shoulder. "Alex."

I twisted around. "Yeah?"

He shoved his phone in front of me. There was a list of Marissa's name on the screen, all from text messages and missed phone calls. "Your girl keeps calling. What's up with that? I thought she had a boyfriend here."

"She does." Eric leaned forward and looked down at the screen. Angie and Justin turned to listen as well.

Angie grabbed the phone and bent over. Her fingers flew over the keyboard before she held her breath and waited. It beeped a second later and she showed me the phone.

Marissa: Hey, where are you?

Angie/Cord: At Haze. Come here.

Marissa: how?

Angie/Cord: Take a cab. Tell the lady u with the g west group.

Marissa: Ok. B there soon.

Angie/Cord: K.

I looked up with a chest full of tension. "What'd you do?"

She shrugged and sat back. I got a glimpse of Angie that I hadn't seen in a long while. She was pissed, she was beyond pissed, and she was calculated right now. Marissa didn't stand a chance.

"Angie, I don't think you should have done that."

"Are you kidding me?" She gestured over her shoulder. "She took off and left him high and dry. She left when we were trying to talk to you about our concerns. She always just takes off and shows up with a new guy. It's got to stop. I'm sick of it."

She had a point, but it didn't sit well with me. Not at all. In fact, after I had taken my third deep breath in a row, Jesse dragged me out of the booth and into a dark hallway. The music was muted slightly, but we were allowed a little privacy. A few people wandered past us, looking for their own boxes.

He pressed me against a wall and stepped close. I felt his breath on me. "What's wrong?"

"Nothing."

I looked away, but he turned my face back to his. He was so close, agonizingly close. My heart started to thump louder and louder. Then he leaned even closer. His lips brushed against mine as he asked again, "What's wrong?"

I started to shake my head. He stopped me.

"Alex."

His lips were on mine now, lightly. But he held back. Desire was starting to build between my legs. It was throbbing down there and I wanted to pull him tight. My arms ached to grab him, but I kept them against the wall. I knew he was tormenting me for information. He had no intention of finishing what he started. Not then, anyway.

"Alex." His breath caressed my skin as he whispered my name. "What's happening? I know something's wrong. What is it?"

"Is that Jesse Hunt?" A female voice sounded from our right.

He went stiff and didn't move for a second.

My hand skimmed up his side to his arm. I was about to ask what was wrong, but he turned and clipped out, "Sabrina."

A high-pitched laugh rang out as she drew closer. She was gorgeous: tall, willowy, with long hair that curled around her waist. And she had striking cheekbones underneath green eyes that looked like something I would've seen in a supernatural movie. Glitter was dusted over her cheeks. It matched her makeup and the glitter in her hair as well. She swept a rail-thin hand in a graceful move over her chest before it fell to her side.

"So you remember me?" she murmured in a husky voice as she drew even closer. Her eyes narrowed at our closeness, but she pinched her lips together in a faint pout. "And who is your friend?"

Jesse's hand tucked me behind me as he stood in front, as if to act as a barrier. Then he asked, strained, "Are you here with my father?"

"Goodness, no." Another high-pitched giggle peeled through the air. "Why would you assume something like that?"

"Because the last time I saw you, my dad's cock was six inches deep in you."

Her laugh dropped to a husky tone again. "Oh. That."

"Yes, that."

"Who's your friend, Jesse?"

"Why?" His hand kept me firmly behind him. He moved again as she looked around him. "So you can report back to my father who my dick has been six inches inside?"

"Has it?"

My eyes went wide at the sharp skepticism from her.

Then he delivered smoothly, "None of your business."

"Hmmm. Something tells me your father will be very curious. He's coming to your game tomorrow."

Jesse straightened again, any part of me that hadn't stiffened at the sight of her snapped to attention at that threat. "Really?"

"And he's having dinner with your coach right now, along with some parents of a dead kid."

He bit out a savage curse under his breath. "Get away from me. Now."

"Jesse—"

"Now!" he barked before he took her shoulders and pushed her away. "I mean it. And tell my father I have no wish for his attendance at my game."

"You don't mean that—"

"I do! Leave."

She hesitated again, but when he turned back to me, she didn't linger long. As she left, a ragged breath left me. His coach and his father were having dinner with my parents. It was all about Jesse, all about Ethan, all about the two of them and their friendship. No one else mattered.

He cursed again before he cupped my face in his hands. "Alex, talk to me."

And then I'd had enough. My parents had left me. The numbness was filled with a different emotion, one that I didn't want to acknowledge. I didn't want to feel. I didn't know if I could contain it.

"Hey, guys," Cord spoke up, apologetic.

Jesse cursed again but looked up. "Yeah?"

He gestured behind him. "Uh, your girl showed up. Things aren't going so well."

"My girl?" Jesse was clueless.

Cord's eyes slid to me. "Her girl."

Her girl? Oh—Marissa. Shit. I shoved past both of them. I was in time to see both of my friends in a corner. Angie raised her arm and swung at Marissa, who ducked to deliver one of her own. I cursed again and hurried toward them, but Jesse's arm went around me. He held me back. I tried to break free, but he wrapped his other one around me, too. Then he yelled in my ear, "Look."

Eric was holding Marissa in the air. She was kicking and yelling over his shoulder while Justin held Angie in the same manner as Jesse did with me. Angie's face was twisted with rage. She tried to leap for Marissa again, but Justin ducked his head, swung her around, and barreled toward us. He grunted as he swept past us, "How do we get out of here? These girls are nuts."

Angie was still glaring and gritting her teeth as she looked at me. The ends of her hair were wet from sweat and she blew out a puff of air so the thin hair over her forehead lifted up. I reached over to move her hair aside so she could cool down. She gave me a sloppy grin and grumbled, "I'm done with that girl. She can be your friend, but she's no longer my best friend.

She's shady as hell. I'm done with her, Alex. I'm sorry, but I am."

A pang of regret hit me in the chest. "I'll talk to her."

"It won't do any good. She's lost it. She's crazy. I swear. Good luck to Eric. She came here reeking like sex and look at him now."

We both looked over. He had her pinned against a corner in the box with his hands on her hips. His head was bent low, whispering something to her, but she couldn't seem to tear her eyes away from Cord. A look passed between the two of them, and a shiver went over me. Cord had been lying to me. I knew it then. I felt it in my gut. She'd been with him during the day, or he had known where she was. He had played clueless with us, but when her eyes darkened with lust and his answered back, a snarl came over me. If she hadn't cheated on Eric already, she was going to. It was only a matter of time before she was in Cord's bed again. And then it was my turn to be disgusted by a friend.

Angie was right. Marissa didn't want our help. I had never cared before, so why did it bother me right then? Even when she went after Jesse or Eric, I had let both of them go without much of a fight. With Eric, there'd been no fight and now I was ready to rip into her because she cheated on him?

What was my life coming to? Why was I caring again?

"Hey." Jesse's arm tightened around my waist. He bent forward and asked in my ear, "You ready to go back? Justin can't hear my directions so we'll have to lead them out of here. Most of the team has already left, too."

I jerked my head in a nod.

"Are you sleeping with me?"

I jerked my head in another nod. I sure as hell wasn't staying with Marissa tonight.

Camden had stayed behind, but when he got some signal from Jesse, he led us out. I could hear Angie whispering to Justin as they walked behind us. He kept hushing her. Eric, Marissa, and Cord were somewhere behind them. Eric, to my surprise, still had his arms around Marissa's waist and refused to let her go, even after I heard her shriek at him a few times. They waited for a different taxi, but I called out, "Cord, come with us."

Marissa swung her head around. She glared at me before she narrowed her eyes, but she kept quiet. I stared back. I didn't care. Eric was a good guy. He didn't deserve to ride in the same taxi with the guy she was going to cheat on him with.

When we got back to the hotel, Jesse let go of me. He followed us as we went back to Angie's room for my bag and then took my hand in his as we went to his room. When we got off the elevator, all the doors were shut, but we could hear the guys' voices inside their rooms. And then, as Jesse was opening his door, his coach came out into the hallway. He ran a tired hand over his face and fought back a yawn. He pulled his robe tighter around him while his bare feet peeked out from the bottom.

"Do I want to ask where you've been tonight, Hunt?"

Jesse's hand curled around my waist and pushed me into the room. "No, you don't, Coach."

He grunted, but replied, "I met your dad tonight."

Jesse stiffened.

"He's an asshole."

"I know, Coach."

"All right. Well, good night. I expect all of the guys in tip-top shape tomorrow, and since it's eleven now, you've made your curfew. Is that girl going to be a problem?"

I stiffened this time.

"No, Coach, she won't."

"You promise, Jesse? I've never seen you attached to a female. This one doesn't bode well with me."

"Coach, I believe you met her parents tonight as well. And they haven't been the best ones to her."

"Oh." All the gruffness was gone from his tone. "Well, all right then. Good night to you both."

"Night, Coach."

"Night, girl."

I stuck a hand out the door and waved. Jesse rolled his eyes, but his coach barked out a quiet laugh before I was pulled inside the room. Then, as the door closed behind us, Jesse turned and regarded me for a moment.

I held my breath. We were alone. There were no friend dramatics, no other guys or teammates around us, and his coach had left us alone. It was only me and him. Jesse dropped his hands from the door and walked to me, quietly. A shiver went up my back as I watched him move with a gracefulness that was sensual and dangerous at the same time. His eyes had darkened. The same desire leapt inside me. It burst into flames, and I gasped when I felt his fingertips against my skin. They trailed around my neck, and he turned my mouth to his. My heart was pounding. It wanted to burst out of me, but then everything went away. I gasped and he lifted me into his arms. Then, I felt the bed sheets underneath me. All I wanted was him. All I needed was him.

17

Jesse was gone when I woke to the hotel phone ringing the next morning. Angie sounded bright and perky on the other end. Apparently my cell phone wasn't doing the job, so she had asked around and found where the Golden Boy's room was. I was supposed to be thankful she hadn't come in person. I almost hung up on her. I wasn't ready for her that morning. I wanted to curl back up in bed and never move. It smelled like Jesse. Everything did—the pillows, the bed sheets, even the towel he had left on the other bed.

But Angie was insistent, so an hour later, I met her in the lobby for breakfast. She looked refreshed in a blue dress with her hair in braids on top of her head. Ugh. She looked gorgeous. I touched the ends of my hair and knew my messy ponytail would never look sexy on me, not when I stood next to her.

"Hey, my only best friend now. What are you hankering for?"

"Jesse," I grunted.

She froze for a second. The bright smile slipped a bit, but she rolled her eyes. "Okay. I got that, you stupid girl-who's-going-to-be-destroyed-later-by-him, but I was talking about food."

I opened my mouth.

"And not in the way of what you want to taste right now, but actual food that we can sit, order, digest, and take home in a doggy bag. That kind, you wanton woman, not anything that has to do with sex."

I closed my mouth. I had another smartass comment on the tip of my tongue, but I sighed. "I'm sorry. I'm still pissed from last night, I think."

"You think?" She arched an eyebrow high as the hostess led us to a table in the hotel's restaurant. As we slid into our seats with the pool as our backdrop, Angie frowned when she opened her menu. "I've moved on to being angry."

I opened mine as well. "But why are we so angry? She didn't do anything to us last night."

"Uh," she choked out, shocked. "Are you kidding me? You don't even know what she said to me last night."

"What'd she say?"

"Well, she called me a bitch when she realized I had been the one on Cord's phone. Then I called her a backstabbing bitch, both to her boyfriends and to her friends. I called her a bunch of other names too, not appropriate for here."

When the waitress approached, we both ordered coffee. As she left, I glowered over my menu. They all looked the same: skinny, gorgeous, blonde hair, with very full lips. I growled as I remembered Sabrina from the night before, and the club's hostess as well. Both could trip on a box of doughnuts and get fat for all I cared.

"Okay." Angie snapped my menu out of my hands and snapped her fingers in front of me. "Where'd you go? I was here ranting about our lost friend, but you went somewhere else. I know you, Alex, and I know you don't have it in you to be that angry at Marissa."

Oh, right. Marissa.

I shrugged. I was beyond caring now. "I don't know. I was

pretty upset with her last night, too. She doesn't treat Eric right at all."

"Hmmm mmm."

"What?"

She gave me a knowing grin. "And that has nothing to do with you and Jesse, right? You're not equating him and Marissa together? She cheats on Eric. He'll cheat on you. You see where I'm going?"

"No." We weren't in an exclusive relationship. He could do whatever he wanted. So could I.

"Oh. Okay, well, you're mad that she'll cheat on Eric?"

"If she hasn't already." I leaned forward. "Her and Cord were giving each other the bedroom look last night."

"Really?"

"You didn't catch it?"

"No." She was surprised, but the waitress returned with our drinks. After the coffee was set down, we both ordered toast and fruit. The waitress seemed disappointed when she left. "I'm surprised that I didn't catch that."

"You were distracted with wanting to scratch her eyeballs out."

"Yeah, there's that." Angie grinned as she took a sip of her black coffee. I poured a creamer in mine as she asked, "So the game is tonight, at six. You're still going with us?"

I shrugged.

I didn't want to open a conversation about how my parents would be there and there'd be a memorial dedicated to Ethan. I couldn't handle that conversation right then and there. "You think Marissa is still going?"

She rolled her eyes. "I suppose. She's the one with the tickets. Crap. I didn't think about that until now."

I laughed. "Wouldn't that suck? You confront her about ditching us and she gets you back by giving your tickets away to someone else?"

She slumped in her chair. "Man, that sucks, but I'd respect her a bit more if she did that. It's something I would do."

I laughed harder.

Angie grinned at me. "What the hell am I going to do? You can't ask Jesse for tickets?"

I shook my head. No way was I going to risk that the seats he'd give us would be next to my parents. He'd do that without thinking, although his comment last night had surprised me. It'd been the first real one he had made that told me he was aware of what my parents were doing, or that I might be hurting because of them.

I swallowed that painful thought away.

She'd been watching me as I pondered all of that. Her eyes were too knowing as she sat back. "Okay. We're not going down that road, apparently." Then she smirked. "Maybe we could call that captain on their team? He seemed like a nice guy, what's his name, Ryan or—"

"Reed," I supplied. "And that'd be worse. It wouldn't be right if we asked him for tickets. Besides, I think it might be too late."

"Yeah, you're right."

Our breakfast arrived and we both ate quickly and then paid at the table. As we walked out, I asked, "So what's on the agenda for you and Justin today?"

Her eyes sparkled in humor. "Can I make a comment like you did? Instead of Jesse, can I say Justin? Would you be okay if I disappeared for the day with my man? We had a crazy dirty night last night. I was worked up. I got him worked up." She pretended to shiver from excitement. "He scratched me right and I scratched him back."

"Okay," I laughed and hit her arm. "Shut up. I got it. I won't bring up Jesse in that way anymore."

She tipped her head back as a carefree laugh came out of her, but it ended on a sour note. We stopped in our tracks when we saw Eric in the lobby. He was on a couch in a far corner with two of his bags packed at his feet. His head hung low, and he was hunched over his knees.

She sighed, "That doesn't look good."

I touched her arm. "Let me, okay?"

"Have at it. Hopefully she didn't railroad him like she does all her guys."

"What?" I mocked her. "What about the ones who leave her in the dust?"

Angie grinned and waved at the same time. "Listen to us; we've turned into the mean girls. Good luck over there."

As she went back to her room and I headed to Eric, regret filled me for a moment. I was being mean to Marissa. I had flinched as I heard the bitterness in my tone as well, but I also knew that everything would work out with her. It always did, even though it might take a while this time. For some reason, I couldn't turn my back as easily as I did before. Her recent betrayals hurt more than they normally did.

"Hey." I sank onto the couch beside him and tapped his bags. "What's up with those?"

Eric's head snapped up. His eyes widened, but then a depleted look filled them. His shoulders sagged forward. "I had a great lie to tell you, in case I saw any of you guys, but screw it. She's not worth it."

A foreboding sense filled me. I asked quietly, "What'd she do?"

"Besides spending the night in Cord Tatum's room?" He shook his head. His mouth was strained at the corners. "She screwed him all night long, and they were loud enough that his roommate had to bunk somewhere else. She loved telling me all about it this morning."

"I'm sorry, Eric." I reached up to pat his arm.

"There's more," he said on a bitter laugh.

"Oh." My hand fell back to my lap.

"Yeah, and I guess this morning he told her to take a hike."

"What?"

"Yep. I guess they party hard after their games, and he said he'd be getting other ass tonight. He told her not to wait for him, and that she should patch things up with her boyfriend. I guess he thinks I'm a nice guy."

The anger rolled off him in waves, but he was tired too. I saw the exhaustion in his depths. Then he continued, "None of that went over well with her. She came back to the room, screamed at me for an hour that I was a horrible boyfriend because I still had feelings for you and she knew it."

He closed his eyes and shook his head. His hands formed into fists. Then he bit out, "She blamed me for everything. She said I wasn't good enough for her in bed, that I was too nice to her. She liked having guys treat her like shit. She said Cord had been *liberating* in bed, that she do him anytime he called her." He cursed under his breath and swung his head toward me. I jumped back at the bleak look in his eyes. "Is that what it's like for you and Hunt? Are you with him because he treats you like crap? Do all girls go for that?"

I sucked in my breath and told myself that this wasn't really about me and Jesse. I started to reach for his arm again, but he hissed as he yanked it away. "Don't touch me, Alex. Don't ever touch me again unless you're going to follow through with it."

"What?" My mouth fell open.

He jerked to his feet. "I mean it. Don't hug me. Don't pat me on the shoulder. Not unless you're ready to follow through and screw me. Isn't that what you do with Hunt? He touches you and you melt for him. It disgusts me. *You* disgust me."

"Eric."

"I mean it. I'm tired of it. I'm always the good guy. I always get crapped on. I'm done with it." He started to turn away but then pulled something out of his pocket. He threw it at me.

As four pieces of paper fluttered in the air, I couldn't move. This wasn't an Eric that I had ever seen before.

He grabbed his bags and glared at me. "I'm going back home. Marissa took off this morning. She said she couldn't stand being around me. I took the tickets out of her purse when she was in the bathroom so there you go, you can still watch your boy's game. Shit." He shook his head again. "I'm still being the nice guy. I wanted to be with you, but you never gave me the signs. And then Marissa was all over me and I thought, 'why not? She wouldn't hurt me,' but the sad thing is that she did. I cared about her. I actually did. And then this trip happened. This was the trip from hell. I got to watch both girls that I cared about fall all over the assholes. That's what he is, Alex. You know that, too. I know you know that. He's going to break your heart. Why won't you stop it? I don't get that. Why do girls like you always go for guys like that? I bet he hasn't even lied to you about it, either, like Cord did with Marissa. He told her upfront that he was going to screw other girls tonight, and I know she'll still go for him if he ever calls her. You do that. You're both so weak. You're spineless." He held a hand to his stomach. "You make me sick. I can't even look at you."

The tickets were lying on the ground at my feet, but I couldn't bend to pick them up. I couldn't even pick up my own mouth as it fell beside them. My feet were cemented in place as I watched him leave. This was Eric Nathan, the good guy who was never going to hurt me. It was then, as I heard everything he flung at me, that I realized I could've been happy with him. He wouldn't have hurt me as I knew Jesse would. He would've been good to me, treated me right. And maybe, even maybe, he might've helped me heal from the pain that I had left at home.

Shit.

He walked away from me, but he was right. Everything he said was right. And even as he left through the doors, I knew I'd still go to Jesse that night. But this time was different. This was the last time. I would end it after tonight. I had to, otherwise everyone would be right. I drew in a shuddering breath. I should've been crippled by what Eric had said to me, but I wasn't. Strength started to fill me. I couldn't explain it. I had no idea why I wasn't crying or why I wasn't filled with shame because he'd been right about me. Maybe it was because I knew I had one more night, or maybe I was lying to myself. Either way, as I finally bent and picked up the tickets, I knew what I had to do.

18

I didn't tell Angie what Eric had said, but I did tell her that they had broken up and Marissa left. I expected a snarky comment from her, but she was silent. She only gave me a repressed smile instead. Justin, perfect timing as always, swooped in to literally sweep her off her feet. She shrieked as she threw her arms around his neck. They bounded away, toward the cab, but I heard her laughter a second later.

And then I followed behind. Since Marissa and Eric had both ditched for the rest of the weekend, I promised Angie that I would still go to the game. I knew Jesse wanted me to come as well, but when we got there, I wasn't ready for the intensity that filled the stadium.

Purple and white were everywhere. There were so many banners for Jesse and Camden, that I couldn't count them all. My favorite was the one that read "Jesse can Hunt me down any day!"

The stadium was packed, and hip-hop music blared from the speakers above, but when the team came out, the cheers were deafening. I cringed at the screams from the girls when Jesse ran in with Camden. Half were going crazy over Jesse while the other half seemed to cheer for Camden. The screams never died down, either, not even when they started playing.

The game was exhilarating to watch.

Jesse was in the zone, and I understood why he'd been dubbed the "Golden Boy." When he got the ball, he made the shot almost every time. After he sunk his sixth three-pointer in a row, the crowd was on their feet in hysteria.

Angie nudged me and bent down. She had to yell in my ear, "Your boy's gotten better."

I nodded with a foolish smile on my face. I couldn't wipe it off. I didn't want to. I was proud of him. He'd been unstoppable at our school, but she was right. He'd doubled his training, and it paid off. That was when I realized why his father was making such a big deal out of him. Jesse was going places. It was no wonder his father wanted everyone to remember whose son he was. More than once, the camera had zoomed in on Malcolm Hunt in the first row, sitting beside my parents. I heard the commentary and knew they were discussing what it meant to have the prestigious movie producer in the building and what kind of career that might mean for Grant West's Golden Boy. One of the commentators remarked they only hoped to hold on to the Golden Boy until the inevitable professionals would take him away. He hoped that wouldn't happen until Jesse finished college, but it rarely happened for an athlete of his caliber to remain until getting a degree.

As I watched the rest of the game, it was bittersweet. I had the same hopes as everyone else in the stands. They loved Jesse, and they wanted him to stay with the team. I knew Ethan would've wanted the same. He would've pushed Jesse to finish college, so because of that, I knew there was a strong probability that Jesse would last until the end of his four years.

I enjoyed the game, or I did until halftime. After the dance team did their show, the lights went back to normal and everyone left for the restroom or concessions. It was then that I looked up to the video screen and saw Ethan staring back at me.

I froze.

His eyes seemed to penetrate me as he smiled. Then the picture was replaced with another of him and Jesse together. Their arms were thrown around each other's shoulders. They wore the same basketball uniform and both looked so happy. Then a third picture came over the screen, this one was of Ethan and his prom date. He was tall and proud in a black tuxedo as she gave the camera a forced smile in her green dress. Then it was him at graduation. He wore his black robe, with his cap and gown in hand. He had flipped the camera off with his middle finger. A few people laughed at that image.

Another was of him and our parents, but more and more pictures showed him and Jesse together. As the slideshow continued, a haunting melody came across the speakers. Then the stadium quieted as so many were pulled into the slideshow.

Angie's hand found mine and gripped tight.

I tasted something wet on my lips and realized there were tears on my cheeks. I'd been crying and I hadn't known it.

The images never seemed to stop. There were so many. Ethan, Ethan and Jesse, Ethan and their other friends, more of Ethan and our parents, Ethan and his girlfriend. I gasped when there was one with me. I couldn't believe my parents had considered that image, but it felt right to see it. More tears burst forth from me. The picture was my last morning with him. It was my birthday, his graduation day, and he had smeared my birthday cake all over me. I was trying to pull away from him as his hand reached past my arms with more cake.

A whimper left me and I looked down. I couldn't see anymore, but a force that wasn't mine led my eyes back. I couldn't look away now. Image after image. All of them were of Ethan and the life he had led. He looked happy in every photograph. He looked content.

Oh God. Why did he die? Why was it him?

Torment and agony sliced through me, back and forth, back and forth. It was as if someone took a butcher knife to me. Each picture, each memory, was another stab deep to my gut. I wanted to bowl over. I wanted to cry until I had nothing left in me. It was too much pain. I couldn't handle any more.

Then Angie gasped, her hand squeezed mine in a knee jerk reaction.

The camera was on me. Blood drained from my face when I saw the tear-drenched cheeks, the swollen look of misery, and haunted eyes. But then I was switched to an off camera, a screen to the side stayed on me, and the slideshow continued of Ethan.

I saw the words scroll over the screen.

In memory of Ethan James Connors, the brother that will never be forgotten. November 24, 1993 to June 2, 2012.

I couldn't stop myself. I shrunk in my seat and pulled my knees to my chest. I buried my head in them as I kept wiping the tears away. But I still couldn't look away. Then I saw that the same camera that had found me in the stands was on my parents across the court. My mom was crying and my dad had his arm around her. Malcolm was next to them. His arm was stretched across as my mom held on to his hand. The only one who was unaffected was Sabrina, who yawned and fanned herself with the program.

I surrendered after that. I didn't even try to stop the tears. As they slid down, I let them go. When the game resumed, there was no announcement of what had happened. I figured the commentators had probably talked about Ethan, who he was in relation to Jesse Hunt, and they probably even realized that I was his sister, but everything else went back to normal. The buzzer sounded and people started to watch the game, but I felt their eyes. People below us snuck back glances. I knew those behind were watching me, and the few in my aisle wouldn't look away. Even when Jesse sank the last shot in and the buzzer sounded, everyone jumped to their feet, but the weight of their gazes wouldn't leave.

As we left the stadium, I was recognized and stared at until we were finally outside and in the confines of a taxi.

And then a different set of tears came out.

Something had happened in that stadium. It was something beautiful that I couldn't comprehend. I had left Ethan inside. I had left a part of me behind, and as we pulled away, I knew I would miss that. I would miss him, but a weird peace came over me. I didn't welcome it, not altogether, but I knew it was there. I knew it was time.

"You okay, girl?" Angie asked in a soft voice. Her hand hadn't left mine the entire time.

I nodded. I missed Ethan, but I nodded to her. I would be okay. I knew it then, and I knew Jesse and I were done. It was time to walk away. I'd been ready before the game, and that feeling was still with me. It hadn't left.

It was time, but I still had my one night.

We went back to Haze. Angie wore a white dress while I wore a light blue one. The fabric was thin and loose. The ends tied around my neck and also under my arms around my back. It had been between this one and another, but Angie had picked the backless dress. She told me it was Jesse-to-die-for and even gave me a wink at the end of that statement. I knew she didn't approve, but at least I didn't feel her disappointment at the mention of his name.

When we got there, I hadn't heard from him, but it didn't matter. We got our drinks and headed to the dance floor. We stayed there the whole night; we moved and swayed when the tempo slowed and sped up. The beat was hypnotic. I was in a trance when a pair of hands slid around my waist. I didn't have to look. I knew those hands. I leaned back against Jesse's chest. His arms pulled me backward and his hips moved with mine. His hands held me in place.

My hair was moved to the side as his lips settled in place. They nibbled on my neck and slowly began to move upwards.

Heat flared within me. As his hand went around my waist and slid down, I gasped. I arched my back against him. My neck was exposed to him even more. He grasped the back of my neck and tilted me farther out. My breasts ached for his touch. I knew he could see them through the dress. He could see them from the top as he had it pulled away from my body. His hand slid underneath and caressed the side of my stomach.

I melted under his touch.

When I tried to turn toward him, Jesse held me in place. His arms tightened around me. We were molded together; every inch of us was cemented to each other.

I didn't want it any other way.

His lips kept nibbling on my neck. His tongue swept out and licked at my thrumming pulse. That sent a rush of heat between my legs, and I pressed against his hand. I wanted it down there. I wanted it to stop the throbbing and fulfill it, but his fingers curled around mine. I felt him grin against my skin and held my breath. What was he going to do? But then he led both of our hands down my side. He slipped them in through an opening in my dress. It flared by my hip and our hands touched the top of my V-string. It was such a tiny piece of cloth, covering almost nothing. Still, he traced his fingers back and forth across the material, making me throb for him. I salivated for his touch. And I felt a deep chuckle reverberate from his chest as he was pressed against me, but then his hand left the back of my head and circled around. It slipped underneath my dress as well and skimmed the top of my breasts.

I shuddered under his touch.

But then he switched positions swiftly. I was thrown around and slammed back into him. He was molded against my front now. My breasts were pressed against his chest. I felt him through his pants and he held my hips in place as he ground against me.

I gasped. All thought left me as I only felt him. I only wanted him.

One of his arms held me up behind my back, but I tipped back. My head fell back and my neck was exposed to him. I rubbed my breasts against him, delighting in the shiver that wracked through him. I couldn't get enough of him.

He held me paralyzed as he bent forward. His lips moved down from my neck and lingered between my breasts. His hand had a cement hold on my hip as we moved together in rhythm to the music, but also to our own rhythm. He kept kissing me, but it wasn't enough. I wanted to feel his lips on my breast. He would catch the tip between his teeth and he would sweep his tongue around it. I wanted him to do that now, but he didn't. He wouldn't go farther. I opened my eyes through a haze of lust. I wanted him now.

He lifted his head, saw the plea in my eyes, and grinned. His hand skimmed up my back. He lifted me back to him so we were pressed against each other once again. I purred in satisfaction. We were so close, only a few barriers kept us apart. My hand slid down and fumbled for his jeans. I wanted it open. I wanted to feel him against me, skin to skin, but he caught my hand and lifted it up.

I mewled in protest.

"Not here, Alex," he whispered against my lips. "Soon."

It didn't make sense. Why not? I wanted him, but then I hoisted myself up. I wrapped my legs around his waist and looked down. My breasts were eye-level to him, but he watched me. The same lust had taken over him. I watched as he tried to fight it, but I was blind to anything else. I wanted him to be blind to it, too.

Then I was ripped from his arms.

Angie cursed and panted as she pulled me away. "Holy hell. You two can't even be around each other in public. I swear you were ready to rip off his pants and sink down on him right then and there on the dance floor. Weren't you?"

I struggled to understand her words. None of them made

sense, but I needed Jesse. So I headed back to him.

"Oh, no." Angie threw me into a room and slapped a hand on the door. The lights were flipped on.

I hissed against the sudden bright light of the bathroom. It was painful and seeped through the trance I'd been under. "What?" I gasped out, still reeling.

"Finally." She cursed again and crossed her arms. Angie propped herself against the door, on top of the garbage bin, her feet thrown up on the nearest sink. She was immovable and stuck her chin out at me. "You're going to cool off for a while."

"What?"

"You heard me."

"I . . ." Fully formed thoughts were a struggle for me. So much was beyond my understanding then. "I—what's going on?"

"Are you drugged?" She raised an eyebrow. "That would make sense, but he was barely holding it in, too. Holy, Alex, the two of you are hot. I almost lost it. I wanted to drag Justin to this room and have my way with him, but I can't leave you alone for a second. Were you really going to screw him on the dance floor? I mean, really?"

"Ugh." A searing pain was starting in my head.

"Don't call me that."

"What?"

"You said I was a pain in your ass. You're going to be thanking me later. People would've had that on video. Can you imagine that? Going to school on Monday, and there's video of you and Jesse Hunt boning on a dance floor? I'm surprised they didn't call security on you two. Everyone was watching. Well, hmmm, maybe that was why. Free entertainment and all."

"Angie," I seethed through gritted teeth. It was painful as reality sunk back in.

"Hmmm?"

"Please shut up."

"Oh. Sure." She shrugged but gave me a fuck-off smile as she switched her legs. When she was more comfortable, she sank back against the door and wiggled her eyebrows. "But, man, that was hot."

"Oh God," I groaned. His hand was under my dress . . . both of our hands were under my dress. I wanted him to touch my breast. Then I was on top of him. I groaned again.

"Yep. Sucks, doesn't it?"

"Stop." I moaned, cradling my head with my hands. Shame coursed through me, filled with regret. I didn't regret Jesse or wanting Jesse, but the place. I wholeheartedly regretted the place. Oh my God. We were in a nightclub. We were in *public*.

"Now will you thank me?"

"Thank you." I glared at her as I did. "Cut me a break. It hasn't been an easy night, you know."

The snarky tilt to her mouth dropped and her eyes widened as she shot off the garbage bin. "I'm sorry, Alex. I am. I sort of forgot about the game and . . ."

And Ethan.

"And everything," she finished.

I jerked my head in a nod, but turned for the sink and splashed some water on my face.

"Don't smudge your makeup."

I looked up. Too late. The mascara was smudged, my concealer was in clumps, and my lipstick had long ago been rubbed off. I was a mess.

"What am I going to do?" I heaved a deep sigh. What the hell was going on with me? I'd been a crying fool in front of thousands and almost had sex in public. Thousands could've seen that, too.

Angie gave me a sympathetic smile and stood in front of me. She flipped the water on and dabbed a paper towel under the faucet. Then her gentle hands took my face as she started to wipe away the rest of my smudged makeup. While she did, she asked, "Can I ask you a question?"

"Sure." I was already at the mercy of her hands.

She hesitated a second but asked, "Why did you sleep with him?"

"What?" I stiffened and opened an eye, but she started dabbing my eyelashes. Then I took another deep breath. I felt the confession building inside me.

"I thought you were going to wait, you know, for a steady boyfriend? And you wanted to make sure he loved you back. Why'd you break that vow to sleep with Jesse?" She chuckled to herself. "I mean, I get it. I do. You two have some damn amazing chemistry, but still, that's what you preached before . . ."

I felt her hesitation again. It stung.

"Before Ethan died," she finished as she started scrubbing the other side of my face.

"I don't know."

"Come on, Alex. You do too know."

"No, I don't. The night we did it, the first night was hard. Ethan had just died and it was his funeral that night."

"I always wondered where you went that night, but I never asked." Angie sounded far away. Her voice was so soft. "That was the beginning when you never seemed with us, you know."

"I know." And I did, because a part of me had died with Ethan. I had ceased feeling grounded, except with Jesse. He grounded me, he anchored me. "So that was the first night, and honestly, it wasn't something I planned. He was hurting. I was hurting. We stayed the night together and everything went away, just for the night. The next morning was a whole other thing to deal with, though."

"So you lost your virginity to him?"

"I did." And I didn't regret it. I loved Jesse. He might not love me, but I loved him and I needed to be with him. Even though it wasn't permanent and had lasted longer than I had thought it would, I would never regret giving myself to him.

"Are you happy that you did that? I mean, he's not boyfriend material, Alex, but you're still with him. The two of you have some weird relationship together. It's not healthy."

"It's not." But I wouldn't want it any other way.

"What about someone like Eric?"

I held my breath. My heart picked up its pace as I waited for her to continue.

She lifted my face and started to wipe underneath my jaw. She cleaned it all up. "You know he'd date you. He's a good guy. He'd treat you right, be patient with you. He would go the extra mile for you and I think you know that. Jesse wouldn't do that for you."

But he already had, in some ways.

I sighed and looked down. What was I doing? Why was I such a mess inside?

She moved away and washed her hands under the faucet. I looked up, and the somberness in her eyes nearly brought me to tears. Oh God. What was I doing to make a friend like Angie worry so much for me?

I whispered, "What do you want me to do?"

"Stop it."

A tear slipped out. Then I nodded.

She added, firmer, "Stop it right now."

"One more night," I gasped out. I needed one more night.

"No." She stood in front of me and grasped my arms. The severity in her took my breath away. It meant so much to her. "No more 'one more nights'. You'll keep wanting that. You'll keep saying that. Stop it right now. We'll fly home tonight. We'll leave tonight. Just stop it with him. I *just* got you back. The old you is coming back. I can see it and I *do not* want him to take it away. He can't take you away again. I won't let him."

I closed my eyes as I heard her words. Pain whirled around in me. I felt ripped open from the inside out. My heart was wrenched out and squeezed so it would stop beating. But she was right and I knew it. I had already started down that path. I told myself to walk away, but I wanted one more night. I needed it so much, but she was right.

It had to end.

I nodded. The relief that came from her almost brought me to my knees. Angie swept me into a tight hug and kissed my forehead. She continued to hold me against her and brushed my hair away from my forehead. It was a motherly gesture, a realization that had new tears come to me, but I held them back.

When we walked outside, Jesse and Justin were waiting in the darkened hallway. A fierce emotion was in his depths, but he wouldn't let me see it. As I stepped closer, he turned away. I sighed, and my hand fell back to my side.

He had heard. I didn't know how, but he had.

"We're going home," Angie murmured to Justin in a hushed voice. He pulled her in for a hug and pressed a kiss to her forehead, the same way she had to me.

"Jesse." My voice cracked.

He shook his head but then whirled back around. His lips were on mine and he kissed me like he was drowning. I raked my hands through his hair and surged to meet him. When he would normally pull away, he didn't. He kept kissing me. His lips were trying to cement his memory on me. I let them. I needed to remember, because I loved him. I didn't know if I would love another like I did Jesse. But then he pulled away and rested his forehead against mine.

I clung to his shoulders, weak and helpless. Everything hurt. It was painful to breathe.

He brushed a hand against my cheek and tucked some hair behind my ear before he whispered, "It's Ethan's birthday, but I understand."

He pulled away. He pressed one last kiss to my forehead and then turned and went back into the club.

A part of me went with him.

19

W hen we got back, Angie stayed with me. It was hard, it was really hard. Jesse and I were done. I knew it was true this time, and the pain crippled me every day, but I heard Angie's voice in my head. Every morning, she said to get up.

"You get up every morning. You shower every morning. And you go through the motions. You do what you're supposed to and someday it won't hurt as bad." I had looked up at her and asked, "Do you promise?"

"I promise. It's better this way. I promise, Alex. I do. You just have to get up every morning."

So, that was what I did.

At first I didn't notice much. School seemed the same. Angie would tell me later that everyone knew about our fight with Marissa. She became best friends with Sarah Shastaine. When I heard that, I was dumbfounded. I thought I would've noticed if Marissa had become best friends with Jesse's ex-girlfriend, but I hadn't. I'd been clueless. Angie told me that I walked through the hallways like a zombie. I was the living dead. And she also told me that Eric apologized to me about something in the first week.

She didn't know what he apologized about, but I had told her that he said he was sorry for something.

I shrugged at that information. I didn't remember. I didn't remember anything anymore.

Christmas passed. New Years passed. Easter passed.

I didn't remember any of it, but I did what Angie said. I got up, showered, and I did what I was supposed to do. I studied and I did it hard. My grades shot up. My test scores went with them and when the school counselor called me to her office to offer her congratulations, it took me five minutes before I comprehended what she was saying.

I'd been awarded a full scholarship to Grant West University for my academics. I was the second student to receive a full scholarship and the third to receive a scholarship in general from there. I already knew the other two, Jesse and Cord.

Huh.

I should've cared, but I didn't. I left the office that day, but I never saw the odd expression on her face or how she reached for her phone afterward.

Of course, there'd been no word from my parents. They were still gone. Where they went, I had no idea. What they were doing, I had no idea, but I knew my father traveled for his job. I guessed that's what they'd been doing, traveling for his job.

I was eighteen; I had been for a year now. They didn't have to tell me a thing anymore.

It was the end of April when Angie asked me a question that I had never considered before.

"Who are you going to prom with?"

My head jerked up. "What?"

Then she slammed her locker and raised her eyebrows.

"Huh?"

"Prom. You. Me. It's in two weeks. Who's taking you?"

"No one." I blinked rapidly, for some reason dumbfounded again. Prom? I'd only been thinking about graduation, well, not really. I still hadn't told Angie about my Grant West scholarship. I'd been holding that in for two weeks, waiting for the right time.

"No one? Are you kidding me? I thought Michael Helmsworth was drooling all over you at the party last weekend."

Oh. That's right. I'd forgotten about the party.

Angie snorted as she slung her purse over her shoulder, along with her book bag. "What? Did you forget?"

I had. "No."

She stared at me with narrowed eyes. "Are you okay?"

"I'm fine."

Then her hand went to her hip. My eyes widened. I knew what that meant.

"Alex." Her voice dropped to the no-nonsense tone. "What aren't you telling me?"

"I forgot about Mike. Really." I scratched the back of my head. "But I thought it was Carl, his brother."

"Oh, yeah." The hand fell away and we began walking toward the parking lot. "So, who are you thinking?"

"For what?"

"For prom." Angie threw her hands up. "I swear that I'm having a conversation with myself here. Are you here? Are you actually Alex? Or did we leave you somewhere I don't remember?"

"Yeah, Las Vegas," I muttered before I realized what I said. Then my hand clamped over my mouth, and I stopped in my tracks. I had not said that. I really hadn't.

But Angie grew quiet and looked away.

I had said it.

When she turned back, I wasn't expecting the tremor in her voice as she rasped out, "I'm sorry, okay? I thought it was for the best if you and he stopped doing whatever it was that you were doing. I didn't expect for you to be like a zombie again."

A baseball formed in my throat, and I swallowed it away. It was painful as it slipped down, but I mustered a tentative smile.

"It's okay, Ang. I was going to end it with him anyway. I just did it ten hours earlier than I had planned. That's all."

"Really?"

I touched her hand and she held on to it tightly. "Really."

She let out a deep breath of air. "Thank God. You don't know how guilty I've felt since that trip, not to mention Marissa." She nodded in the direction of the person in question, and Marissa straightened and glared back, but her eyes flickered as they rested on me for a second. Sarah Shastaine cleared her throat behind her and Marissa turned her back to us.

That was the most interaction we'd had with her since Thanksgiving break.

"Ugh," Angie growled. "She drives me crazy."

"Yeah, that happens when people suddenly drop out of your life with no explanation." There was heat to my words and I was surprised at myself. Where had that come from?

"What'd you say?"

"Nothing."

"Oh. Okay. Well . . ." We approached the parking lot now and she paused by the door. "If no one's asked you, then I think you should ask someone. What about Eric?"

My stomach dropped. "Like hell." He already had chewed me out once. I wasn't giving him another reason to do it again. Eric and I were better left forgotten, like everything else in my life.

"Okay." She grinned. "But he asked Justin about you at baseball practice. He wanted to know if you were still with Jesse."

"Really?"

She nodded and then pushed through the door. The sun was blinding, but the air immediately rushed at us. The air conditioning inside was cool, but I warmed up as soon as we took another step outside. "So I think you should go to his party with us tonight. Talk to him there."

"Talk to Eric?"

"Yeah. He and Brianna broke up. Can you believe he dated

that cheerleader?" She snorted. "Although, I think he did it to piss off Marissa, since they're on the same squad together."

"Good," I murmured. I meant it.

"Yeah . . ." Angie's eyes had taken on a thoughtful look to them. She was biting her lip.

I readied myself. She had something on her mind and she was going to say it. I knew the signs like the back of my hand by now.

"So."

Here we go.

"What happened to your parents, Alex?"

I forced my tone to be casual. "What do you mean?"

"I mean . . ." She looked around and inched closer. Her voice dropped low. "The counselor called me into her office today. She said she'd been trying to reach your parents, but she can never get a hold of them."

"What'd you say?"

"Nothing. I mean, I don't know anything. I know they went on that trip, but to be honest, I haven't seen them since. That's weird, Alex. Really, really weird. Are your parents around? Please tell me they're around."

"My dad travels for work. You know that."

"Yeah, but he wasn't gone all the time. He was gone some of the time and your mom was always around. How is she, anyway? I come over twice a week, and you're always alone."

I jerked a stiff shoulder up. What lie would sound normal here? I didn't even care enough to actually lie. "Just leave it alone, Ang. Okay? I don't want to talk about my parents right now."

"But—"

"I mean it." I interrupted her. I shouldn't have to cover for my parents or lie and tell everyone that they'd basically abandoned me. That wasn't my lie to tell, that was theirs, and I had some pride not to cover for them.

"Okay." She held her hands up in surrender. "I won't bring 'em up again. Promise."

"Good." That was what I wanted, but why didn't I feel good about it?

"You work tonight, right?"

I nodded.

"When do you get done?"

"I close with Ben at nine tonight."

She chewed at her lip. She was thinking again.

I sighed, "What is it?"

"I'll come over at nine thirty. Will you be ready by then?"

"What about Justin?"

"He's got the baseball game. Some of the guys want to start as soon as they're done, so I figure I'll be driving tonight anyway. I'd rather take my car."

"Or I could pick you up, and you can drive his car home? You don't have to worry about both your cars."

"Yeah." She bobbed her head in an easy agreement. "That sounds like a plan. See you at nine thirty. Maybe bring Ben?"

Both of us laughed at that idea. If I knew my co-worker he'd be bouncing up and down at the idea of going with us. He proved me right when I asked him at the end of our shift. He was clapping, giggling, and planning his outfit at the same time.

We got to Angie's late because Ben made me pick him up from his house first. He wanted to "bond" with the girls and he wanted a ride home that night. When Angie got in the car, his clapping and giggling happened again. He wiggled his eyebrows in the air and announced how excited he was to get drunk that night. He was hoping for a little titty twister from his "lush babies." Angie and I never asked who he meant, but I had a good suspicion that I'd find out by the end of the night.

When we got to Eric's house, I was surprised at how long it had been since my last time there. His home was a white, two-story, ranch-style home. The front patio wrapped around the house and I saw that the rooms were as big as I remembered.

Someone ran into Angie, who glared. "Excuse you."

The person flipped her black hair over her shoulder and revealed her face. I didn't need to see who it was. I already knew it was Marissa. Only she could wear a brown tank top with black cropped pants and look hot in it.

She'd been laughing, but that vanished immediately. Her eyes went dead and she straightened. "Excuse you."

"No." Angie blocked her as she started to go around. "Excuse you, bitch."

Marissa drew back. Her jaw stiffened, her mouth flattened, and she tightened her grip on her cup. When she started to move her arm back, I hurried and got between them. I knew Marissa's signs, too. No one wanted anyone throwing cups tonight.

"Hi, Marissa," I rushed out with a fake smile. "How are you?"

She paused, confused, but her arm went back to normal.

"Oh. Hey, Alex." She was wary now, but she sipped from her cup.

I relaxed and shooed Angie away before I turned back to her. "So are you dating anyone?"

Her eyes narrowed. "What do you mean?"

I could hear Angie and Ben bickering behind me, but then Angie huffed out, "Fine!" She stormed off. Ben gave me a small smile before he bounded after her.

"Look." I dropped the façade. "I didn't want you and Angie to have another round."

Her smile was bitter now. "Oh, you mean like the last eight times since Las Vegas."

"Eight?"

Marissa snorted. "Where've you been, Alex? It's a normal thing for her and me to get into it. It wouldn't be a party if Angie and I weren't screaming at each other. There was hair pulling at the last one."

"Really?"

She rolled her eyes. "I thought you were getting better. What happened to you? You slipped back into the land of the dead. Are you able to graduate? Did you get all your studies done?"

"I got a full scholarship to Grant West."

It took a second before I realized what I said. Then I gasped, and my mouth dropped open. I couldn't believe that had slipped out. I hadn't even told Angie yet.

Marissa's eyes bulged out and she was quiet for a second. Then she whispered, "Holy shit, Alex. Really?"

I nodded, still in shock.

"Wow, that's, wow. That's great. Congratulations."

I nodded again. Everything started reeling around me.

"So, you'll be with Jesse then? Like, for real? You guys can be a couple."

Everything fell flat again. I shrugged as I responded in a monotone, "We ended things in Las Vegas."

"What?" she squeaked. Her hand clamped on to my arm. "Are you serious? The two of you are done?"

"Have been for a while," I said through gritted teeth. "You and Cord?"

"Oh." She waved a dismissive hand in the air. "He's been back twice. We hook up, but that's it. I'm not stupid. Cord's like Jesse, they're not relationship guys. He tells me about all the girls at their college. They have groupies there. Can you believe that?"

I nodded. I really could.

"Yeah, I guess you'd know, huh?" She sipped her beer and gave me a shy smile. "I got into Hurley College."

"Oh. Congratulations."

Her eyes sparkled. "Yeah, me and Sarah. We're going to be roommates."

"Oh." Pain speared through me. She had replaced Angie and me so quickly. "That's good for you then."

She nodded, biting her lip now.

"Isn't it?"

All the happiness, all the excitement left her. Sadness flooded her next, and she heaved a deep sigh. "Are you okay, Alex?" She edged closer to me and gripped her cup tighter. "I know things didn't go right between me and Angie, but I never stopped caring about you. I know Angie's your best friend. She's always been closer to you than me, but I'm just worried. Are you okay?"

Oh no. We'd taken a nosedive into the emotional and things I didn't want to talk about. I shook my head and started to back away.

"Alex." She hurried after me.

"No, stop." My insides twisted around each other. I needed to get away from her. I couldn't hear anything more from her. She'd left me. I couldn't handle taking her back.

"Alex."

"Stop." I turned and darted through the crowd. Angie and Ben were in the kitchen. I knew they'd be getting drinks, so I turned down a far hallway and ran into a hard chest. I stumbled back, but before I hit the wall, an arm snaked around my waist holding me in place.

"Hey, Alex." Eric set me on my feet and bent so he was eye level with me. He gentled his voice. "You okay? You look upset."

"Everyone is so damn worried about me," I snapped out.

He straightened abruptly. His blond hair was gelled at the tips, giving him the just rolled out of bed look that was intentional. With a loose white tee shirt over ripped jeans, Eric could've been a model.

And holy hell. When did I start noticing him in that way?

I cursed under my breath before I squared my shoulders back. "I'm sorry, Eric."

"Hey, no problem." He lifted his cup in front of him and raised his eyebrows. "I'm just here, drinking, hanging out at my place. Have you been here before? Wait, you must've."

"Your seventh grade birthday party."

His cheeks reddened, and he made a point to drink from his cup. Then he coughed. "Yeah, that's not embarrassing. We did our seven-minutes-in-heaven thing, didn't we?"

I couldn't stop a chuckle at that memory. We had been shoved inside, but it'd been the longest and shortest seven minutes of heaven in my life. "You kissed me on the cheek."

"I did?" A wide smile appeared. "I was aiming for your lips. I was trying to be aloof and mysterious. Did it work?"

I shrugged, but my stomach fluttered as I remembered the feel of his cool lips. I'd been so excited. I had pulled Angie into the closest bathroom and squealed about my first kiss on the cheek. "I had a crush on you back then."

His eyebrows shot up again. "You did?"

I nodded. "Yeah. I did. You were a big deal."

"I can't imagine I was that big of a deal."

"You were the most popular guy in our grade." Still was.

"Yeah." He quieted, gave me an awkward look, and reached up to scratch the back of his head. "Maybe. No one could compete with your brother and Jesse."

"They were a grade older."

"I know, but I knew that all the girls liked those two. You included."

A rush of heat went to my cheeks, and I knew I was blushing. I just shrugged.

"Yeah, you guys were close." He frowned. "Didn't he live with you guys at one point?"

I nodded. "Yeah, from eighth grade to the end of his junior year. His mom died and he pretty much moved in with us. His dad was always away."

"I remember seeing him at your place all the time."

My eyebrows lifted.

He hung his head slightly. He confessed, "Justin, me, and Troy rode our bikes past your house all the time. Troy and I had big crushes on you. Justin always wanted to see if Angie was over at your place."

Warmth flared inside me again. It was the good kind; it'd been too long since I remembered my past like this. It felt right. "Yeah, that's right. Those two were always fighting and picking on each other."

"Now look at them."

"Yeah, I know. The first couple to get married, I bet."

"Yeah," he laughed. "Probably." And then the mood shifted.

I grew tense, but the ends of his mouth dipped down. He looked tired all of a sudden, and he let out a breath of air. "Have you been okay, Alex? I know it might not be my place, you know, since the last time we really talked I ripped into you, but I still care about you. Are you okay?"

I held my breath and nodded. My throat had gone dry and there were butterflies in my stomach. I hadn't felt like this since, well, since Jesse. Then I gulped again. My throat was so dry. I needed something to drink. I grabbed his cup from him and finished the rest of it. Then I shoved it back into his hand. He hadn't moved.

"Oookay."

I flushed. "I was thirsty."

"Oh. Well, stay here. I'll get some more beer for us."

Panic took over, and I grabbed his arm when he started to go. "Don't leave." I stopped, surprised at the fear in my voice. My hand fell away, but I couldn't keep quiet. "Don't leave. You'll go. Someone else will come. I'll feel weird. This is nice, right now. You and me. This is nice."

"Okay." He said it gently as he touched the back of my elbow. "We can go to my parents' back patio and talk. No one should be out there. I'll have someone get us something to drink. Actually, I think my dad has a liquor cabinet in his closet." He gave me a sheepish look. "We're not supposed to know about it since they don't want us to drink, but we always did."

"Of course." I relaxed then and my knees were weak from the relief.

"Okay. Through here." He guided me into a back master bedroom. "Hold on."

I waited in the darkness as he moved away. Clothes hangers were pushed aside, he cursed, and then there was a loud thud on the floor.

"Eric?"

"I'm okay," his voice came out muffled. "My mom's got so many damn clothes. I can't find the light switch in this stupid closet. Oh, here it is."

Light flooded the room then and I blinked from the sudden brightness. But then as my eyes adjusted, I saw a king-sized bed with cream bedcovers. There was a desk area with a couch behind it and three floor-to-ceiling bookcases filled with books. When Eric emerged from another doorway, he lifted his hands as he wiggled his eyebrows. He had two bottles of Boones Farm.

"Huh? This is the good stuff."

I burst out laughing.

"Or I could mix us some drinks. My dad's got everything back here."

I struggled to stop laughing as I asked, "Why does your dad have a liquor cabinet in the closet?"

"Oh." His grin turned into a fond one, and he shrugged. "My mom doesn't drink, but my dad likes to have one every now and then. My mom would only allow it back here. She's pretty strict with her religion. Sounds stupid, I guess, but that's my folks. Sometimes I think this is their little haven away from us kids."

"Yeah, it could be a little studio apartment."

He gestured toward the desk that had a flat screen television hanging on the wall next to it. "She likes to do her work over there. Dad will kick his feet up and watch television some nights when he wants to be around her."

"Your parents sound like they have a good marriage."

"They do." Then he nodded toward a back door. As he held it open and I slipped past him, he added, "I think they designed their room like this on purpose. All of us kids get free rein of the house most nights."

"You have two little sisters?" I frowned as we sat on padded lounge chairs. I should've known how many siblings he had. I'd grown up with him.

Eric placed the two bottles on the glass table in front of us and stood back up. "Yeah, two little dorks and I have two more brothers. Isaiah is two years younger than me and Noah is four. I think he was an 'oops,' but he's so darn cute. No one can resist him. He's going to get the ladies when he's older."

I shot forward when he reached for the door again. "Where are you going?"

"I'm going to mix us a few drinks. These things were a joke, but feel free to open one if you'd like. Be right back."

When he came back, he slid a glass toward me and I took it for a sniff. I couldn't get a whiff of any liquor so I took a sip of it. It was mostly soda, but he had put a small amount of alcohol in there. "Thanks."

And I felt grateful to him for another reason, a deeper reason, but one that I couldn't explain. The ball of tension that was always in my stomach unraveled a little bit. It loosened up, and as it did, the rest of me started to relax more and more. Before I took another sip, I knew I wouldn't want to be anywhere else at that moment. This was just fine with me.

He tried to look casual, but I saw the delight on his face. He lounged back, kicked up his feet on the table, and threw an arm on the back of my chair. He raised his glass to me in a salute. "Here's to us being friends again."

"I'll cheers to that."

As our glasses clinked and our gazes locked, a tingle went through me. It'd been a long time since I had felt one of those, since my Thanksgiving break.

20

"Are you and Eric going to prom together?" Angie flopped on her bed and lifted the remote control to silence her television.

I was at Angie's house for Thursday night dinner with her family, which had become a weekly occurrence. Her home had become a second home to me. I plopped on the small couch she kept in the corner and pulled a blanket over my lap. I shrugged. "I think so, but I'm not sure."

She sat up straight, giving me a meaningful look. "Are you serious? You two have been attached at the hip since last Friday. Everyone's saying you two are dating. I know you're not, not yet, but really, Alex. Call him right now and ask him."

"No." I squealed and then laughed. I couldn't believe I had squealed. "Oh, my gosh. I haven't done that in forever."

Angie smirked. "About damn time, too."

I giggled into the blanket and fell over. More laughter came from me. Oh God. It felt good to laugh.

"Come on, you nut." But Angie couldn't hold back a grin. "Call him."

"No."

"Come on."

"No." I shook my head. I was stubborn.

She groaned and fell back on her bed. "You drive me crazy. Can I call him, at least?"

"No."

At her glare, my shoulders shook some more in silent laughter. But then I changed the topic. I wasn't ready to deal with whether Eric was taking me to prom or not. It felt surreal to me, for some reason. What she said had been true. We had spent every day together for the last week, and that night we sat up and talked until morning. At six, we went to the diner with a few others for breakfast and he took me for coffee when everyone went to their own homes. When I had gone home, there was a text from him after I woke up. He wanted to take me to dinner and we went to the movies afterwards. Every day was something new. Sunday had been a walk in the park. He picked me up for school on Monday and drove me home after his baseball practice. I cooked dinner Tuesday night for him. Wednesday night had been movies at my place. It was Thursday now and I was excited for the taco place he promised was the best in town. I had never heard of it, but I wasn't the best source for anything.

As a dramatic sigh left her, Karen hollered for us to come down for dinner.

Angie muttered as we went downstairs, "I can't believe you're not staying. You always have dinner with us these nights."

"I know." I hopped off the bottom step and grabbed my purse by the doorway. I poked my head in the kitchen. "I'm off, Karen. I'll see you next week!"

"What? You're not staying?"

Angie's mom was tall and willowy like her daughter. She had the same blonde hair, which ended in the middle of her back. While Angie's eyes were a smoky blue color, her mother's were a bright sea blue. She was golden tan and the wrinkles around her eyes were the only indication of her older age. Then she gave me a radiant and loving smile.

"I already told you, Mom. She's got a date. She stopped by to say hello because she feels guilty if she doesn't come over now."

"Oh, come now." Angie's mom waved at me and winked. "I'll package some food up and you can take it with you on your date. I'm sure whoever he is will be hungry."

"They're going out for food, Mom."

"Oh, well—" But her words were cut off short as Angie's little brothers and little sister raced into the kitchen at the same time. Soon chaos ensued. Plates were dropped on the floor, spoons were flung across the room, and someone started crying. Angie collapsed on one of the chairs and lifted pleading eyes to me. "Can I come with?"

I gave her a farewell wave and left before Karen had time to bag up any food for me. I still had the leftovers from last week in the refrigerator. But when I got to my car, Angie yelled at me from the door. She rolled her eyes as she hurried toward me with a bag in her hand. "My mom made me do this. Sorry. Have fun on your date. Ask him to prom." Then she turned and darted back inside.

I groaned. It wasn't that easy. A person didn't open their mouth and ask someone to prom, even if you had been spending every day together for a week. A week. That wasn't very long. Not at all. Oh, who was I kidding? I was terrified when it came to my love life. No, I was petrified. That was more accurate, but when Eric picked me up, there was a whole host of butterflies in my stomach, which I didn't think was a bad thing.

"Hey." He smiled warmly at me.

"Was I supposed to dress up?" His crisp buttoned-down blue shirt was tucked inside black jeans that looked more like dress pants. Glancing at my shirt and jeans, I felt dowdy.

"No, no. I had a thing today. I came straight from that, but you're good. You look gorgeous, like always."

"Really?"

"Yeah." He pressed a kiss to my cheek and urged me toward his truck. "You ready?"

"I am, if I'm dressed okay?"

"You are, I promise."

"Okay." I smoothed out the front of my shirt and my jeans as we went to his truck. After we climbed in and he pulled out of the driveway, I asked, "What thing did you have today?"

"Huh? Oh." He frowned. "Um, just nothing really."

"What was it?"

He shrugged and reached for the radio, turning up the music. The same old dread started in my gut again. It had doubled and tripled by the time we got to the taco place, and when we pulled into the parking lot, I felt ready to burst.

"Okay, we're here. Sammy's Tacos. You've really never heard of this place?"

He sounded so carefree and nice. The stone in my gut told me otherwise, and I sat there without a word. My chest started to heave up and down, and I already knew my heart was pounding like crazy. I just sat there with my arms folded into my lap and my hands twisted around each other. What was I supposed to do? But then it didn't matter. We weren't dating. We were hanging out. He had said that he wanted us to be friends again, but this Eric felt different from the one before. He had more confidence at his party, and he didn't seem so genuine anymore. I remembered the nice Eric, the one that would never lie to me or turn the radio on so I wouldn't talk.

"Alex?"

I shook my head.

"What? No, what?"

I couldn't believe I asked myself this, but what would Angie do? What would Jesse do? I knew both of them wouldn't stand to be dismissed like that. So, I swallowed hard and looked up. This was going to be hard, maybe harder than I would ever realize.

"Alex." His eyes were now flat and impatient.

"Screw it."

"Excuse me?"

I had said that softly, but I said it louder this time. "Screw it."

"Screw what?"

"You."

"Me?" His eyes widened. "What did I do?"

"You hushed me."

"I hushed you?"

"Yes, with the radio." I turned to squarely face him and tucked my hands under my legs. My heart was still pounding, but my voice had gotten stronger. I could do this. I could express to him what I was feeling.

"What?" He frowned and scratched his head. "Are you sure?"

"Yes. I asked you a question. You didn't want to answer it, so you turned the radio on. You did that so I wouldn't ask you again. You hushed me."

"Oh."

He was still struggling to figure out what he had done. A pang of sympathy went through me. He had no idea he'd done it. That meant he had done it before, maybe with Brianna. I tried a different way. "You never talked to me about Brianna."

"I was supposed to?" His eyebrows went high and alarm crossed his features.

"No, I meant maybe you did that to her or she did that to you or something?" The confusion on his face doubled and I sighed. Maybe I wasn't saying it right, but then I started to wonder what I was even saying in the first place. "Never mind. I'm hungry."

"Great." He was visibly relieved as we got out and headed into the taco place.

It was a small, but quaint restaurant. Large Mexican hats and sombreros were on the wall, along with newspaper clippings of bull riding events. Fake cactuses were set in the corners of the room, along with stuffed snakes and one armadillo.

As we slid into a window booth in the front, raised laughter from the back caught my attention. I turned and looked for the source over my shoulder, and it didn't take long for me to find it.

A rail thin girl stared back at me. Her eyeliner was smudged and her lipstick had been rubbed from her lips. She sat up straight and flipped her dirty blonde hair over her shoulder as she narrowed her eyes to see me better. Then the bathroom door swung open and closed. Jeremy Benson walked through as he scratched his chest idly with a big yawn on his face. He wore the same military style buzz cut and he looked tired. But as he saw Barbie's scrutiny, he looked at me, and I gulped. Surprise and delight flared in his depths, replaced with something darker.

"What's wrong?"

Eric was frowning at me with a menu in hand. The waitress was beside him, both looked concerned.

"Nothing."

"Oh. Do you know what you want to drink?"

"Oh. I don't care. Diet soda."

Eric's frown deepened, but I couldn't help it. I was speaking fast, and I wanted to be gone from there. A boulder lodged itself on the bottom of my stomach and I had an intense desire to call Jesse, but then a hand was slapped down in the middle of our table.

"Well, lookie here." Jeremy grinned at me and twisted around to study Eric with the same smile. "Who is this, Jesse's Girl?"

"That's Eric Nathan." My voice came out as a squeak. I swallowed again and forced it to sound stronger. "His dad is a cop."

Eric's eyebrows shot up as he looked from Jeremy to me. "Who are you?"

"It don't matter," Jeremy said smoothly before he turned and leaned against the table with his back to Eric. He scooted closer to me and dropped his voice to an intimate whisper. "Are you trying to scare me away, Jesse's Girl? Or aren't you Jesse's girl anymore? He seemed real protective of you. Did that change? I'd sure like to know what happened to change that."

My eyes were firmly attached to my lap. I couldn't say anything. I couldn't move, but when I felt his finger touch my arm, I jerked away from him and almost out of my seat. Jeremy just placed his hand on my shoulder as he laughed. "Well, steady there, Jesse's Girl. I was only asking you a question. You don't have to get all spirited like an old horse or something. I ain't cornering you with ill intent. We're all friends here." His smirk deepened and something dark flashed in his eyes as he included Eric in his last statement.

Eric had tensed up. His eyes were hard and his jaw was firm, but his gaze lingered on me for a moment before he slid off his stool.

"Oh, whoa, hey." Jeremy made a show of backing away from the table with his hands up in surrender. "I'm not here to start anything."

"You're making her uncomfortable."

"Yeah, well, I can see why she might be." He winked at me as he regarded Eric again. Jeremy swayed his body around. He was loose and having fun, while Eric stood as rigid as a statue. "Oh, come on. Like this ain't funny. She's Jesse's girl, man. You have to know about that. He damn ripped my head off last time I saw this little bitty—"

"Come on, Jer." Barbie stepped forward and grabbed his arm. "We're already late."

"I'm having fun."

"Let's go," she snapped at him. "We're real sorry, but we have to be going."

"Oh, come on." Jeremy protested as she dragged him out the door, but we heard her snap again, "She's Ethan's sister. Leave her alone."

Anything else Jeremy was going to say was cut short. And then the door swung shut behind them. The table was quiet; I couldn't get her words out of my head. A longing filled me now. It was so deeply rooted in me that I hadn't known it was there. I thought I was getting better, but I wasn't. Then I shot out of my chair. I needed to know about Ethan. I had to know.

"Alex!"

I ignored Eric and shoved through the doors. Barbie had gotten Jeremy in her rusty truck and as she was rounding to her side, she saw me coming. She froze in place. Her eyes widened, and fear flashed over her before she tried to hurry to the driver's side.

"Wait!" I called out. She didn't, so I sprinted after her. "Wait!" I slapped a hand on her door as she tried to pull it closed.

"Let it go, little girl." Her eyes held a soft warning in them. "Let us go in peace and we'll leave you alone."

"You knew my brother," I spat out.

Jeremy was laughing so hard, his body was jerking in spasms.

"We did." Barbie lost her fight, but turned to Jeremy. He quieted his laughs so they were more silent, but he wiped the tears from his eyes.

His shoulders kept shaking forward.

She turned back, disgusted, and slid out of the truck. "Come on, let's walk." As she shut the door, she gave him a stern warning. "You stay, Jeremy. I don't want any bullshit."

"I won't. Promise." His hands lifted again in surrender, but the giggles that escaped him didn't lend him credibility.

She took a deep breath and then turned toward me. "Come on."

I followed her at a cautious pace as she went back to the taco place and sat down at a picnic table. There were four more, but all were empty and her truck was far enough away so I knew Jeremy Benson wouldn't be listening to us. I was relieved at that, but the wariness that came over Barbie had my stomach twisting again.

Would it ever end?

She sighed and hung her head. Her hands fell in her lap and she seemed defeated as she sat across from me. "I'm real sorry about Jeremy. He can be an asshole sometimes, and I think he likes to torment you because it's his way of sticking it to Jesse. He and Hunt aren't real friendly, but they put up with each other. I guess."

"How did you know Ethan?"

She looked up with tears in her eyes. I didn't know what to say. So, I didn't. She started again. Her voice was raw from the memories. "Ethan became friends with us at the end of his senior year. He never said anything, but something was going on with him. We all knew he wasn't happy. We didn't know if something was going on at home or with his girl. We thought it was his girl because he took up with me."

I couldn't breathe and my chest was starting to hurt, but I was on the edge of understanding something important. She was Ethan's girl?

"We messed around a few times. Hunt wasn't real happy. He never said why, but he and Ethan seemed to fight a bunch at the end. I mean, don't get me wrong, they were always tight. Those two were so damn close. I knew it pissed Jeremy off. Jer liked Ethan. He liked him a lot, but Jesse always came around looking for Ethan, and Jer and him just got to become enemies." She wiped at her eyes, but her head hung down again. Her blonde hair was in clumps as it cascaded around her. I could barely see her anymore.

She continued, but I heard the tremor in her voice. "Anyway, Ethan was hanging out with us all the time. It was nice. He was a gentleman. He never did drugs like the rest of them. The only thing he ever did was drink, but he never got drunk. He was rare, you know." She sniffled. "There are so many dirt bags out there and he was always real nice to me. He even told me about you once." Her head lifted and she gave me a soft smile. Her lip quivered. "He loved you lots. I could tell. Him and Jesse would fight about you, too."

"What?" My eyes went wide.

She shrugged. A faraway look came over her. "No one knows what they fought about that had to do with you; just that they did. Ethan didn't like something and Jesse did, that's all we could tell, but then it didn't matter. The night he died, he was with us."

I couldn't breathe. Oh God.

"He'd been with me that night. He was always so gentle. I felt loved, like one of those types who get their prince in the end. It was nice. I wasn't used to that from guys. I guess that's why all of us loved him so much. He was a good friend to Jer, too; he even got him to stop fighting. And that says a lot. Jeremy loves to fight, but he stopped for a while because Ethan asked him to."

It hurt. Everything was starting to hurt again.

"But he got a phone call from Jesse and he took off. That was the last time we saw him. The next thing we knew, he was dead. I couldn't believe it. None of us could. We tried to go to his funeral, but your momma wasn't having it. She barred us from the place. We couldn't even go to his headstone. I'd like to go sometime. I think Jeremy snuck out there one time, but he never told me. He took a flower from Herbert's pot, but when he came back, he didn't have it. That wouldn't be a big thing with a normal guy, but Jeremy never gives girls flowers. When he came back, his shoes were all muddy, so were his knees, and he had that 'off' look in his eye. I'd know he was thinking about Ethan when he got that look."

When she ended her story, she was sobbing. I couldn't do anything. I didn't even want to comfort her. All of it hurt so damn much. I told myself to breathe. Breathe in and out. Let it go. Exhale. Angie's words came to me then.

You get up every morning. You go through the motions. You do what you're supposed to and some day it won't hurt as bad.

I sat there and breathed until it didn't hurt as bad. When I could finally lift my head, I was jolted to see the haunted expression on her face. She reached over for my hand. As I gave it, she held on to it tightly. Then she choked out, "You had a good brother, you did. He was one of the best. I know Jeremy seems like a scary jackass, but he ain't. He loved your brother like his own and I know he'd take care of you if you ever needed it. You don't need to be scared of us, I promise. I'll set him right. I think he was trying to scare you because he's still mad at Hunt. He blames Jesse for Ethan's death, though we know that ain't right. Jesse was with his girl that night. Ethan told me that Jesse had some family dinner with the in-laws. That's what we called them because we all teased Jesse about being wifed-up, ya know? I'd been hoping he would've come out to party with us. Those two together were fun to watch. They would bicker like a married couple, but you could tell they loved each other. With guys nowadays and all their egos, they don't know how to be friends with each other. Anyway," she squeezed my hand before she let it go. "You say hello to Jesse for me, would you? That'd mean a lot to me."

She got up and left me then. There was so much to comprehend. I couldn't figure it out. I was still sitting there, trying to do that when I heard her truck pull away. I didn't hear when Eric sat across from me. I had no idea how long I sat there, but he would tell me later that he ate our tacos. Then he waited another half hour before he tried to move me. I think I went into shock after Barbie's revelations. The only thing I could do was breathe, only breathe.

21

I never told anyone about what Barbie said to me. Eric questioned me to make sure that Jeremy Benson wouldn't be a problem. I always reassured him; I believed what Barbie had said. I saw the pain in Jeremy's eyes, but I also saw the hatred he had for Jesse. Things still didn't make sense to me, though. What had Ethan been unhappy about? And my parents never said a word about Ethan's other friends to me. They knew. My mom had banned them from the funeral, so they obviously knew about them.

No one told me. No one had said a word.

And Jesse . . . he had called Ethan that night. What had he said to him?

I tried calling Jesse after that. I tried every morning and every night, but he never picked up. I left so many messages, I lost count of them. He was avoiding me.

He didn't respect me, whatever we had, enough to answer my questions.

But I refused to let his rejection send me into a tailspin again. I'd been numb for so long, too long. Angie was right when she said my old self was coming back. I was starting to laugh. I was starting to care about things. I was even nervous about prom (Eric finally asked me), and he made sure it was my own fairy tale. He and Justin got a limousine. They picked us up at Angie's house. Karen fretted over me as if I was a second daughter. She took picture after picture until Angie pleaded for it to end.

And that night was spent in a hotel suite. We shared it with Angie and Justin. Ben also had a date. Each of us had a bedroom that was attached to the suite, but most of the night was spent laughing or in the Jacuzzi. Angie asked me in the bathroom if I was going to have sex with Eric. She said he wasn't expecting it, but it was prom. It was almost tradition.

I laughed at that. My life was not traditional.

Eric got some cuddling from me and made it to second base. That was it. I'd given my all to Jesse and was only now able to breathe normally again. Through the rest of that night, I remembered how Barbie had said Ethan was a gentleman. Eric was as well, it was something that brought tears to my eyes at times. Maybe I was trying to replace Ethan with Eric, maybe that was why I told him that I'd never feel for him what he felt for me.

Eric took it well. He said it was the gentlest way a girl had let him down. And then he said he would still like to spend time with me. So for the rest of the school year, he picked me up for school. He drove me home. We went out for dinners and movies. He would hold my hand in the hallways and carry my books for me. He always knew I didn't feel the same, but after I kept insisting that I didn't want to lead him on, Eric pressed a kiss to my forehead. He told me that he only wanted to take care of me. So I let him. We spent almost every night together over the summer. He would sleep at my home on the weekends, on the bed that Jesse had used growing up.

He never said a word about my parents' absence. Some nights Angie and Justin would come over. The four of us would make dinner and laugh all night. It felt right to have that in my home again. At times, I would feel Ethan's presence next to me. I would imagine he was smiling and laughing with us.

It was the beginning of August when I received a letter from my dad.

Eric saw who it was from and pressed a kiss to my forehead before he went into the living room. I sat down at the kitchen table with my heart pounding and hands shaking. It took me three times to open it. When I did, I almost wished that I never had.

DEAR ALEXANDRA,

Your mother and I received a phone call from your guidance counselor, Mrs. Farm. She was very polite, but forthcoming that our noncompliance to her initial phone calls had been disappointing. Your mother and I have discussed this and have come to the conclusion that our absence from your life has not been fair to you as our daughter. While we are overjoyed you will be attending Grant West University, we feel it is only right that you receive the proper financial compensation from us. You are an adult and have been since last summer, but we have started a trust fund for you. You will receive an allowance every month in your savings account. It will last as long as your mother and I are alive. Ethan stipulated in his last will and testament that his trust fund, in total, would go to you as well. There is another trust fund that your grandfather set up, which you will receive when you turn twenty-five. The amounts are provided below:

Your monthly allowance: $ 2,000.00

The total trust fund from Ethan: $2.5 million

The trust fund from your grandfather: $2.5 million

We feel this amount of finances will provide for you throughout your life. On a personal note, your mother has been doing very well. She attends individual therapy and a grief group therapy session every week. I've retained a life coach to be on our staff. If you would ever wish to contact us, feel free to give us a call. We are very proud that you will attend the university your brother had been accepted to previously. Please give our best wishes to Jesse. We love him like a son.

Best wishes, your father.

I CRUMPLED the paper and then smoothed it back out. A burning sensation grew in me as I sat there. Everything was so clear, so focused. My heartbeat slowed to a steady beat, and I no longer had to remind myself to breathe. I shredded each piece of that letter. I didn't know how long it took, but I didn't stop until each piece had been folded, ripped, folded again, and ripped once more. I finally stopped when the letter was a pile of pieces so small they could've been ash, and then I got up from my seat and went into the cupboard for a lighter.

As I approached the letter my heart slowed. I wanted to enjoy this. I wanted to be turned on by it. I lit it on fire.

As it burst into flames, I stood back. Amazed. I wanted to see it grow more and more. I wanted the entire house to burn around me. Everything my parents had been would be in pieces at my feet. I wanted to destroy them, but I only destroyed the letter. It was a small, empty triumph. I knew my parents would never care. If I mailed the letter back to them, they would only throw it out. Nothing touched them anymore. Ethan's death had done that to them, it was now done to me.

Nothing would touch me again.

Eric rushed into the kitchen, panicked. When the fire alarm had gone off, he ripped himself from the doorway. He then dumped a bucket of water on the small fire. As he did and a cloud of gray smoke filled the kitchen, he fell against the wall. "Jesus," he cursed.

"Don't curse."

"What?" He gaped at me, pale and sweating from the smoke.

I didn't answer him. I didn't care to answer anyone anymore. Everything changed that night.

I never did anything different, but I knew I wasn't right anymore.

People grew distant from me.

Eric stopped spending time with me.

I never heard from Marissa again.

Even Ben asked when I was quitting the Coffee Hut. He sounded like he couldn't wait for my resignation.

The only one I saw two more times was Angie. She came over to say good-bye the day she and Justin were leaving for college. Both of their cars were packed. Justin waited in his truck, parked behind hers, as she came into the house.

I looked at him from the doorway, but he averted his gaze. I still saw it. Fear.

I didn't blame him for staying in the truck. I even understood it. I understood why everyone stopped visiting me. Something wasn't right with me anymore. I knew that, but all I felt was the cold. And rage. I now had so much rage in me, too much to control at times. I had been abandoned. I was haunted. And all I wanted to do was destroy everything.

So it made sense why Justin stayed in the truck. Even Angie couldn't hide how her arms trembled or the nervous twitch in her eye. As she said her good-bye, she couldn't say it fast enough.

I stood and watched them go.

They all left.

And then I turned back to the house to finish my own packing. I was leaving for Grant West University the next morning.

This is the end of Broken and Screwed.
Continue to Broken and Screwed 2
WWW.TIJANSBOOKS.COM

ACKNOWLEDGMENTS

Wow!

I wrote Broken and Screwed so long ago. I've had it re-edited and proofread so these acknowledgements are new. This book, wow. I wrote it and it came out in 2013. I'm writing these acknowledgments in 2020 and I still remember the day I decided to write it, and the night I published it. It was so early on but some days just stick with you. This book was one of them for me.

So my acknowledgements is for the readers who continue to read Jesse and Alex's story and continue to keep them alive. You guys amaze me, and I'm continuously so grateful to those readers.

- Tijan

CPSIA information can be obtained
at www.ICGtesting.com
Printed in the USA
BVHW031803100321
602204BV00002B/156